THE STAINED GLASS WINDOW

A FOOTPATH TO PAINS END

DON GADDO
KIMBERLY DRONZEK

Palmaya Publishing, North Carolina

THE STAINED GLASS WINDOW

ISBN: 0-9707087-0-X

Library of Congress Control Number: 00-93698

Published by:

Palmaya Publishing
Box 773
Chapel Hill, North Carolina 27514

Printed in the United States by:
Morris Publishing
3212 East Highway 30
Kearney, NE 68847
1-800-650-7888

Dedication

There is one person, among many, whose tremendous encouragement helped me along the way with The Stained Glass Window. Thank you, Mom, for all of the time and love you took to help me find my talents and use them in this book.

Kimberly Dronzek

For the members of the 398th Bomb Group who did not return and for those who miss them still.

Don Gaddo

How like an angel came I down.

– Thomas Traherne

Wonder

An American Maiden at Nuthampstead

I was thinking today of pals far away,
In the days that we flew long ago.
I was longing to see the crew faces with me,
Memories fading so.
In the midst of it all,
Did this vision befall,
(The reason for bringing me there.)
"Twas a silver clad maid,
That ten flyers invade,
Her virtue not tarnished at all.

Since first I saw her on the tarmac,
Some camouflaged, some silver clad,
A generation change, improved upon,
A ladies cosmetic fad.

She was that picture perfect.
Viewed as some phantom of delight.
Her graces all became her.
She was envy in my sight.

Regal as she sat waiting missions,
Frustrated awaiting engine change,
She pouted as her engines billowed,
Her nose aloof 'til out of range.

She was proud yet quite forgiving,
Foster children she loved them all,
Like the goddess that she was
Resolute and valiant to her mission call.

Yes, I still see that shapely form
Her memory cast upon my mind.
As she taxies out for takeoff
Tips her wings to those left behind.

That triangulated "W"
An emblem she proudly wore
I still see on wing and stabilizer
Of each B-17 on tour.

Wesley G. Eatchel, Tail Gunner, 398th Bomb Group, 603rd Squadron

This Is Our Prayer

O God the Father of us all, accept our true devotion here today.
From those of us who incline the head to those who kneel to pray.

We hold in sacred memory those in thy hand you now caress.
Who gave their all for freedom in an hour of distress.

That tear that wells up in one's eye with condescending grace
Is but a lighted candle in the reflection of that face.

The cause was not diminished when through the skies he flew,
As the mighty Eighth laid bare her arm with an emancipating view.

Holding fast to a mother's prayer was not to be that day
As God designed the plotted course through the maelstrom on the way.

His spirit then ascending reaching angels there on high.
Was carried to thy bosom in spite of reasons why.

May those of us yet living, to our progeny yet to come.
Never forget the price he paid upon the altar of freedom.

Wesley G. Eatchel, Tail Gunner, 398th Bomb Group, 603rd Squadron

The
Stained Glass
Window

INTRODUCTION

THE LEGEND

"There is a land of the living,
and a land of the dead,
and the bridge is love . . ."

Thornton Wilder

Joseph Doglio was twenty-one years old when he lost his life during World War II. He was a Second Lieutenant and navigator on a B-17 Flying Fortress named *Angel.*

There were unusual stories about *Angel* and her crew. Mysterious stories.

The maintenance ground crew chief for *Angel* in England, Mark Dixon, had experienced uneasy feelings about the plane . . . *"There was something special about Angel and the men who flew her,"* he often said.

One of the stories concerned a teardrop that appeared near an eye on the painted face of *Angel*. A teardrop that was not painted by a human hand.

Then there was the London romance between Joseph and Anne Howard . . . The story about the locket she gave to him and if it still existed today. The intrigue of their time spent at St. George's Church in Anstey, England, is remembered by those who knew them. I secretly wonder what became of Joseph's St. Christopher medal.

There was the mysterious appearance of red roses . . . and the partially opened window in the Doglio home, after Joseph's remains had been returned for burial.

There was sudden recollections of religious passages the crew had written near their battle stations in *Angel* . . . visions and dreams by associates of the *Angel* crew and their families. There was page twenty-seven of the co-pilot, Lieutenant Earl Harts college play script.

Joseph Doglio was my cousin. I was six years old

when he lost his life while on a bombing mission over Lechfeld, Germany. I was fascinated by the stories told to me by many friends and former members of the bomb group. Every story stirred my interest and pushed me to learn more about his short life.

The Stained Glass Window is not only a memorable continuation of the legend of a crew and their *Angel,* a B-17 Flying Fortress but it is a rekindling of World War II stories through the veterans who knew the war well.

It is a week long account of my journey to understand my cousin and the men who fought along side of him.

Finally, it is also the continuation of a chaste love affair that hauntingly endures the passage of time.

The Stained Glass Window is an open window to our dreams and imagination. More importantly it is a window of faith, reality, and a reminder that the decent things in life never die.

3

Chapter One

The Trip

Twirling around to face my worn brown leather suitcase, which has been a comfort to me on many of my most memorable journeys, I begin to list in my head the things that I will need on my next event-filled vacation. This trip isn't the type of vacation complete with white sanded beaches, chilled cocktails and warm sunshine awaiting me, but alas I hope it to be a learning experience and possibly a life experience I will come to treasure. I prepare myself to venture to England for an entire week of planned events. I go, not as a tourist, but as a listener and pupil to learn from those who are older and wiser and know about the interest and topics that have recently begun stirring inside of me.

The idea of the trip began with my cousin. I had heard my older cousins name mentioned many times before and have never known his entire story. Joseph

Doglio was the brave navigator of a B-17 Flying Fortress who gave his life for his country during World War II. This is all I know, because I have never had the opportunity to meet him. I was younger then and couldn't yet comprehend the war or what it stood for. Now, fifty-six years later I find myself planning to accompany close to one hundred of the veterans, relatives and historians whose interest or involvement in the war brings us together. We are to tour Cambridge, Anstey, and Nuthampstead all places that hold memories for the Americans who came to preserve freedom.

One event is the dedication of a window composed of intricate, brightly colored stained glass to forever remember the men of the 398th Bomb Group once stationed at Nuthampstead. My cousin is one of those men. Two hundred and ninety-two souls are to be commemorated in this week for their valor and bravery and their commitment to freedom and their country. Base 131 in Nuthampstead, England, became a second home to these airmen and to many who now have the opportunity to return. This week should be tearful and moving. For some of these veterans, this will be their first time returning to the base and for some it may be their last. I can only anticipate the stories of these veterans, who knew my cousin well and all who knew the war.

The squeaking of the drawers interrupts my thoughts as I pull out the neatly folded shirts and pairs of socks that will be needed for the trip. I never realized how organized my wife kept me until I began packing for my trips. Everything is always in its place from the miniature bottles of shampoo to the shoe polish that kept my favorite pair of brown loafers intact during the rainy walks that I have taken across the globe. Having had the opportunity to travel fairly frequently, my past job as an executive of an international consulting firm kept me venturing to foreign countries and taking more flights than necessary in a lifetime.

After retiring at the ripe age of fifty-five, I found interests in things outside of the business world; World War II becoming one of those interests. I learned of an incredible B-17 Flying Fortress, known as the Angel, and her crew and discovered a little more about my cousin. The men in this crew intrigued me. I yearned to know more about Joseph, Earl Hart, Dallas Hawkins, John Cosco and the other members of the crew and those stationed at Base 131. Even at my seemingly older age, I still look up to these men in admiration and respect them for their courage. I became curious wanting to know who these young men in 1944 were, and what it was like in the middle of a deadly and dangerous war. That is how I came to my decision to take this trip. I felt something secretly telling me that the only way I was to find out about the past is to relive it through the eyes of the veterans, those who truly experienced the event in its entirety.

My thoughts are interrupted again not by the

squeaking of drawers but by the approaching soft footsteps of my wife. After a tiring debate on the pairs of slacks I should take, she leaves me muttering under my breath but smiling at the fact that she still cares about the most insignificant things after forty years of marriage. My eyes gaze over to the clock on the wooden dresser its bold red figures telling me it is getting late. I decide to make room for my tired body on the bed and move the suitcase carefully to the floor. Almost fully packed for the trip, I throw in a few good books for the flight over and review my mental checklist of things to pack. My wife, Kathryn returns from her oversized chair in the living room, her tattered book in her left hand, her glasses gently in her right hand and retreats into bed. I can tell she is excited for me to have this experience in England, but that she is sad to see me leave again. The look she expresses on the nights before I left on trips is one I could never erase. Her eyebrows crinkle in a concerned upside down V-shape and it appears as though she has lost her favorite belonging and is in distress. Kathryn never comes on these long trips of mine, for her fear of flying prevents her from entering any terminal except to find her devoted husband at the arrival gate each time.

As I begin to fall asleep slowly drifting into a dream, I envision the war photograph of my cousin, his crisp uniform and intent face staring at something that only he could know. He had dreams I am sure. Dreams of flying and navigating and owning the bluest skies that ever existed. It was a shame that he didn't live long enough to discover most of those skies. But, for those horizons he did know back in 1944, there is no doubt that he owned them. Hopefully, I can come to understand him and those other brave two hundred ninety-two souls once stationed at Base 131. I long to learn from those who knew the skies of the war and lived to tell their stories. I continue to be intrigued by the mysterious events that followed the crew and their families. I am curious if I will find answers to these puzzling incidents.

Drifting deeper into an anxious sleep of heavy bombers, fighter planes, and men in uniform I am awakened to a familiar voice quietly ringing in my ear.

"Honey," she whispers, "I'm really not worried about you taking this trip, because I think it will be good for you...I have this strange feeling..." I roll over to face her a little shocked at the abruptness of her comment. She is smiling, the moonlight catching her brown eyes, her eyebrows relaxed and not in their normal tense stance. For the first time in years, she appears calm and unfettered by the fact that I will be leaving for a week and flying over an extremely wide ocean for several hours. I can only return her smile and gently kiss her goodnight. I am left with the last words she spoke as I drifted again into sleep. . ."I have this strange feeling." The heavy bombers, fighter planes, and battles once again become figments of my dreams as I anticipate my flight to England tomorrow afternoon.

Chapter Two

The Arrival

At 5:20 in the afternoon, I am scheduled to leave from Raleigh, North Carolina on a non-stop flight to London. There we would take a bus to Cambridge where the festivities are to begin. Making myself comfortable in the seat for the almost seven hours in flight is next to impossible. Planes never have enough leg room and the person behind you always seems to annoyingly nudge you from time to time when they shift their legs trying to become comfortable themselves. I couldn't help but notice, as I was boarding, an older couple a few rows behind me that looked to be going to London with the tour as well. I couldn't manage to find out if they knew of the 398th during the flight and instead retreat into reading a John Grisham novel. Halfway through the book, I begin thinking how surreal it is that I am going to visit the places my cousin had flown during his missions. Amazingly, I am getting the opportunity to experience the countryside and places he had trained so fervently to go.

My curiosity for this young relative began a few months earlier with a small worn suitcase. I had been visiting family in South Wilmington, Illinois and met David Doglio, the distant nephew of Joseph. He had been talking about how he could never find all of the things Joseph had left behind before he went to England. His navigator certificates, pictures, and memorabilia had been missing for many years and as he was describing the missing items, I became intrigued by the memory of my cousin. At my anxious request, David and I began a long, tedious scavenger hunt for any trails of Joseph's life. I happened to see the corner of a tattered suitcase hidden by the edges of a large oak dresser. David said it was empty and been sitting in that spot for years, but the black tape that intertwined and wrapped around the edges of the grayish-black suitcase made me wonder if it was in truth sealing something secret. We both decided for my peace of mind to pry it open and much to David's disbelief and my awe, a treasure we discovered inside. The instant it was opened photographs drifted onto the tops of my worn leather shoes and there was no mistaking that they were of Joseph. Letters, report cards, plaques, navigator charts, and articles from newspapers dated from 1944 gave us insight into a man who had not lived long enough but had accomplished so much in his years alive. One letter on creased blue stationery was to a woman in England. It was never mailed. I was captivated by the words written to this woman known only to me as Anne Howard, for they were loving and simple and I wondered if she was still alive somewhere and still remembering him. In the letter a mysterious locket is mentioned. It appeared through the letter to symbolize Joseph's devotion to this woman as he writes that it will protect and remind him of her love. I wondered if the locket was still out there, possibly still worn around the delicate neck of this woman who undoubtedly cared for him as much as he appeared to care for her.

The plane loses a little altitude as we are crossing the Atlantic and my thoughts drift again from the book to what I will do in Cambridge. Overhearing the chattering of the passengers directly next to me, I casually listen in on a few conversations about how green it is in England and how much there is to see. I glance down at my watch realizing that we have only been in the air for a mere three hours. Deciding that sleep might be the best way to pass the time, I page a stewardess to bring one of their small cloth covered pillows to my seat and attempt to ignore my chattering neighbors and take a nap.

Suddenly startled, I am awakened to the captain announcing in a boisterous and baritone voice that we are an hour outside London and our expected arrival time is now close to 8:00 A.M. The friendly stewardess must have noticed the groggy half-asleep look I now had, because she comes over smiling and offering a hot cup of coffee. I graciously took the cup and sipping slowly I think of all the people I am about to meet in the 398th Bomb Group. There is so much opportunity to learn about Joseph and the war during this trip and I don't want to miss out on any part of it.

I am blessed to have a window seat and as we begin to descend to the runway, I can immediately notice the greenness of the country. The blood is once again circulating through my tired legs as I walk through the terminal to the baggage claim. The coffee had helped a little, but the flight had none the less been long and tiring. The adrenaline begins to revive me as I realize I am now in London and my adventures are about to begin. It took a few minutes to be checked by customs before I make my way to find my luggage and eventually figure out where I was to meet everyone on the tour bus. I notice, after gathering my bags, the old couple from the plane. Their eyes look concerned; their faces are contorted in panic-stricken expressions. I confidently walk up to them and ask if they needed any help. The woman, dressed in a crisp navy pants outfit appears more worried than her husband

and explains that their baggage has not arrived with the others. She is afraid she and her husband would miss the bus they are scheduled to take to Cambridge. I then realize that they are with my same tour group and feeling terrible about the complications that I, too, had experienced many times before while traveling, I stay with them. It doesn't bother me that the three of us are

lagging behind the group. I can sense by their relieved expressions that they are happy that someone was staying to help. Knowing that I will be one of the youngest people in the tour group, I feel an obligation and privilege to be of service to this special veteran and his wife.

Their luggage finally arrives on the carousel, after being blocked in the conveyor belt, and after casually introducing myself to this lovely older couple, I come to find out that Ed Soule had been a member of the 600th bombardment squadron as a ball turret gunner. He and his wife Bea came to London to pay their respects to those he had known and chase memories with those who are still living today. I am in awe of this close couple from the moment they boarded the plane in North Carolina. I just hadn't known that they were here for the same reason I am.

The three of us rush to the awaiting bus and breathlessly I sit in one of the last seats towards the middle of the bus. Next to me is an older man who kindly smiles at me as I squish into the red cushioned seat. It is much more comfortable than the seats on the plane, and I am happy to be on land again. I now can look out the window and truly see the countryside.

The hour-and-a-half ride from London is not enough time to take in everything on the drive to Cambridge. The landscaping looks as though a fuzzy green carpet has been rolled out into large pastures. Gently rolling hills provide an escape from the flatness of the terrain and are covered with patches of wheat, barley, and rape. Wooden fences enclose sprawling green meadows filled with cows and complement the quaint villages and towns we pass through on our way.

Glancing a few rows ahead I notice Ed and Bea Soule animated, giddy, and laughing about all the fun they used to have years ago. It is as though the ride is an elixir to the old veterans. Looking around me, I see the passengers coming to life as we approach Cambridge. Smiles and laughter echo through the tour bus as war stories and memorable past times surface into conversations between people who seem like reunited old friends. I can not believe, as exhausted as I was, how they can be so animated and alive after the long flight. I stop staring at the people in the bus and again turn to glance out of the window. Narrow cobblestone streets lined with mulberry trees greeted me as I am told by my smiling neighbor that we had reached Cambridge. It is almost as I had pictured from the books I had read about England as a child. It is mid-day by now and the sun is brightly shining through the trees and onto the shops. Colleges and universities are visible from the roads displaying exquisite British architecture spanning over almost seven hundred years. People are strolling through the streets going into the small shops and boutiques near the marketplace on Trinity Street. Impressive lush gardens line the River Cam as people in boats casually "punt" down the dark blue water. I am suddenly anxious and ready to walk around and absorb the town on my own.

Pulling into the circular driveway of the Crowne Plaza Hotel, the bus hisses to a slow halt and I am relieved to breathe in fresh air. The hotel, with its Corinthian style columns, looks more like the Parthenon in Athens than a British hotel. The tour group files out and gathers in a semi-circle around Wally Blackwell, the president of the 398th Bomb Group Memorial Association, and the designated coordinator of the week. A few hours are designated to either relax from the trip or stroll the streets before dinner which is scheduled at the hotel at 7:00 P.M. sharp.

I retreat up a spiraling brown marble staircase and past a lobby where two smiling hostesses kindly direct me to my room. After considering a nap, I decide that I will sacrifice sleep so that I can personally experience Cambridge. Changing into some comfortable white sneakers, I walk past the smiling hostesses who tell me that there are some neat sights on the southern edge of town. Taking long strides toward the center of the town only a short walk away, my thoughts turn again to Joseph and the members of the Angel crew. I wonder if they had seen this town and what it had meant to them. Maybe it was a haven they had visited during time spent between missions. Then sadly I remember that they had spent only fifty days in England before flying their fifteenth and final mission. In time I would learn more.

Colleges and enormous medieval churches surround and engulf me as I continue to casually stroll the streets. It is a magnificent sight, the emerald green lush meadows combined with the ancient and worn stone buildings that had weathered through the centuries, and yet remain intriguing to the eye. Cambridge is full of history. Each building, house, and street has its own story to tell to its visitors. I pass a small pub and notice a worn wooden sign loosely swinging above its doorway reading in faded red letters Tally-Ho. I smile remembering what those words had meant to the British during the war. It was what the spitfire pilots would yell as they dove on enemy aircraft. The small pub inadvertently reminded me again why I had come to Cambridge. I had a newly discovered obsession to learn a more personal side of the war.

Passing the pub, I continue to stroll the streets and come to a park bench. Its worn green paint is chipping away from years of tourists, students, and tired souls. I chose to sit on the shady side of the bench to cool down from the sun and notice an older man sitting at the other end of the bench his face gleaming with perspiration as he intently stares at the shops. He looks familiar possibly because there are many older men on the tour in Cambridge. Believing him to be in his late seventies, he conservatively wore a navy collared shirt and tan colored pants. I wondered how he could bear the heat at his age, but he looks as though he is enjoying sitting on the bench, so I hesitate interrupting his thoughts.

"Hi, are you by chance here with the 398th commemoration tour? You look very familiar." His wrinkled eyes turn to glance at me as if he didn't know I am speaking to him. He boldly replies, "Yes, in fact I was a pilot here in the 602nd squadron at Base 131." The thought of striking up a conversation with this man crosses my mind as war questions anxiously begin to run wild through my head. I could immediately tell by his proud stance as he moved closer to sit beside of me that he will be intriguing to speak to. After introductions and explaining why I am on the tour, I discover the man's name is Hank Rudow. His eagerness to share his memories and stories concerning the war magically transform the once silent staring man on the park bench into a jovial, outgoing man who seems to become years younger as he continues to speak. I listen, afraid of missing any parts of the captivating stories that he is telling in such detail it feels as though I could have been at Base 131 myself. He speaks of an incident back in June of 1944 where the clouds and fog couldn't keep him from being the first pilot to take off for a bombing mission over Germany.

The "soup", as they called it, enveloped the base. The group had been ordered to hold their positions on the flight line until the weather cleared. Hank had just arrived in England and he sat in his pilots seat nervously awaiting word from the control tower. Then, mistakenly observing what he thought was a green flare signaling the all clear for take off, he roared down the fog shrouded runway and once airborne he took his B-17 through the layers of clouds. He was on his way to Germany. As he anxiously circled the skies, he noticed no other planes breaking through the clouds into the traditional V formation. Becoming worried and knowing that he was nearing enemy territory, he flew towards the designated rendevous point which was over the English Channel. All of a sudden, an entire formation of B-17 Flying Fortresses came into view and he cautiously decided to join them. Glancing at the large formation of B-17 heavy bombers Rudow was astounded to see that he had joined, not the 398[th,] but the 100th Bomb Group. The 100th had a large square "D" on their tail sections. The 398th had a large red triangle "W" adorning the tail of their aircraft.

Despite his confusion he decided he had come this far and despite his anxieties he was determined not to abort the mission. For this days mission he would be a member of the 100th. He proudly completed the mission and the 100th Bomb Group affectionately called the fortress with the red triangle "W" the ugly duckling. Returning to base Rudow didn't understand where his squadron had gone until he landed and discovered from an angry officer that he was the only one to take off because the weather was unfit for flying. Rudow had been told to never abort a mission and when mistakenly observing what he thought was a green flare he was on his way. Although he was reprimanded for his ignorance, he explained boldly that this mission had been one of the greatest moments in his life.

Occasionally, as he is speaking, people walk by carrying shopping bags and smile at the old man whose enthusiasm is visible in the way he waves his animated hands in the air as he speaks. We sit together on the worn bench for over an hour before he regretfully departed to the hotel to prepare for dinner. Lagging behind I remain on the worn green bench lost in thought. The town is incredible. The smell of flowers, freshly baked bread, and ripe fruit coming from the marketplace lingers in the air. I think about Hank Rudow and his passion for life and the excited look he had when we discussed visiting Base 131 this week. It seems as though he is coming home for the first time in many years as his eyes had sparkled as he spoke about the missions he had flown from the base.

I hear a chime in the distance coming from King's College Chapel and look at my watch to check the time.

By now it was 6:00 P.M. and only an hour until the sit down dinner with the group back at the hotel. I want to stay longer at the bench watching people and creating a permanent mental picture of the town, but I know that I need to go back to the Crowne Plaza. After a brisk walk to the hotel, I shower, changing into a nice collared shirt and the slacks that only yesterday my wife had begged me to bring, and walk downstairs to the Orchard Room where dinner is to be served. Around one hundred fifty people are in the room all talking and remembering each other from years past. All of the people on the tour are required to wear a little rectangular name tag in order to help everyone remember each other, and I sit down at a round table with a man who had known my cousin all to well. John Cosco is the only remaining member of my cousin's plane, *Angel*. He hadn't flown on the crew's last mission because he was recovering from serious wounds received on a mission to France. His entire crew had died in that mission he missed one tragic day over Germany. He had to remember it all. As he is sharing stories of missions and his crew, the emotion overwhelms him and at times his aged blue eyes well up with tears. The table is silent as he speaks and his wife Rosemary occasionally takes his hand and smiles proudly at her husband who so bravely served his country. It isn't until after nine o'clock that the delightful and delicious dinner is finished and people begin to retreat to their rooms. It has been a long and eventful first day and I can tell that most of the people on the tour are exhausted. I am among those people, as I slowly creep up the staircase to my room and await some peaceful sleep. I sit quietly in the room with the television softly stirring in the background. After taking off my worn brown shoes, I lie down remembering Johns tear stained face and thinking how emotional the next few days are going to be for the veterans. Tomorrow, we are to visit the Cambridge American Military Cemetery.

Chapter Three

The Cemetery

The next morning I awake to my alarm clock buzzing with the voice of a British radio DJ telling of the dreary conditions outside. England is known for its numerous cloudy days and today as the group plans to visit the Cambridge American Military Cemetery, the weather seems fitting. The bus takes us to Madingly, which is north of Cambridge. As the bus pulls into the cemetery, an uncomfortable silence erupts; its passengers gazing solemnly out the windows. The cemetery is the only World War II cemetery in the British Isles. Hundreds of alabaster white crosses arranged in perfect symmetrical and circular rows stand on the north slope of a small hill. Woods encircle the edges of the grounds and provide peacefulness to the area. The group exits the bus their faces transforming from the previous days jovial expressions to ones of reverence and respect. I walk in long strides through the grounds joining in silence with John Cosco and his wife occasionally stopping to acknowledge a cross that bears a friend's name. No words are exchanged during these pauses just the kind looks and tearful glances at those souls names etched in stone and remembered in honor by an old soldier. The expression in the old veteran's eyes makes me wonder if he is thinking why he was the only one spared from that perilous mission over Germany that forever changed the course of his life. I can sense that it had been a hard thing for him to accept even after fifty-six long years.

I notice small American flags marking the graves of the airmen of the 398th scattered across the cemetery. While at the cemetery the widows of the 398th Bomb Group ceremonially and reverently place a wreath at the flagpole.

Venturing into the teakwood doors of the memorial chapel on the grounds of the cemetery with John and his wife, I realize there are five pylons each symbolizing a year from 1941 - 1945 in which the United States participated in World War II. Above the entrance etched in a pediment read the dedication: "To the glory of God and in memory of those who died for their country 1941 - 1945." As each visitor enters the hallowed and sacred chapel their eyes become sorrowful and withdrawn for the hundreds of men who sacrificed their lives. People come into the main room of the chapel first looking up at the ceiling. Gasps echo through the room as an impressive mosaic design of the Archangel trumpeting the arrival of the Resurrection and the Last Judgement decorates the sprawling ceiling. Intricate designs in the shapes of B-17 Flying Fortresses, ships, and numerous angels adorn parts of the ceilings above a stone altar. These mosaics are symbolic of the men in the naval and air forces who are buried in the cemetery. Two hours pass until the group is gathered again at the bus and the next destination is to be forty miles away at the small town of Saffron-Walden. Here we are to eat lunch at The Eight Bells pub, a five hundred year old establishment alive with spirit and enthusiasm emulating from the gracious and friendly owners. The pub has several rooms. As is the case with most English pubs, there is a room for drinking ones favorite ale and a separate room designed for conversation. The decor of the room provides a perfect atmosphere for gathering. The furniture is heavy and rustic and the far wall is adorned with a medieval looking fireplace. The remaining three rooms are reminders of a time gone by. Giant tapestries hang from the walls. They are joined by elk heads and grouse. One can not help but imagine that they are sitting in an old hunting lodge. These rooms are used for dining. Just before leaving the friendly meal, Jeanne Stange, widow of Ray Stange a navigator of the 603rd squadron raises her glass. She boldly stands up and in a shaky voice toasts the table. "God Bless the 398th and the men who we loved so well." The chorus of people in the restaurant proudly repeats the toast in unison and clink their glasses together.

In the evening, a reception is scheduled at the hotel for English friends and visiting friends of the 398th. I change into a white button down shirt and nice "trousers" as they call them in England and rejoin the group in the Orchard Ballroom. The room is crowded and bustling with the conversations between veterans and family members remembering old missions and reliving tales of fighter planes and bombing sites. A man in a crisp brown suit approaches me introducing himself as Lord Dimsdale. He owned the land in Nuthampstead in the 1940s where Base 131 is located. His demeanor is friendly and open and he ends our conversation speaking of the base and how different it is today. The tour of Base 131 is not until tomorrow, yet the enthusiasm Lord Dimsdale expresses for this sacred place causes me to want to drive out to the site that very instant. I remain at the party talking again to Hank Rudow and John Cosco and wandering into different circles of veterans and acquainting myself with the group. My eye catches the figure of a woman standing on the opposite side of the room. The light of the chandelier above her casts an iridescent glow on her cream skirt and I notice she is looking in my direction. As I wonder who she is here to remember or to meet, I move slowly and nonchalantly to a circle of men including Lord Dimsdale, near where she is standing. I knew she had noticed that I moved but she continued to stare at the group of chattering men. Forgetting about the woman, I become engrossed in a humorous conversation about an airman who couldn't keep his bunk clean and was reprimanded when his belongings were thrown out of the Nissen Hut and when he returned tired from a mission his bed and things were missing. After the group heartily let out a laugh and remembered their own home away from home at the Nissen Hut, I look over to the window where the women had been standing and she is gone.

Feeling thirsty, I walk to the bar and order a tall glass of ice water. A sudden chill causes my heart to quicken as a soft silk sleeve brushes against my arm. I turn to face a woman whose features radiate a strange kindness. She smiles ordering a beverage in a soft-spoken voice and then turning to face me asks, "You are Joseph Doglio's cousin right?" I am caught off guard that she knows who I am, and I stammered. "Yes I am, may I ask what your name is?"

Her voice is now more confidant and as she speaks her eyes are piercing mine. "Emily. My name is Emily." I am interrupted by John Cosco who requests that I come meet a veteran who had been close to Joseph while they were stationed at the base. I glance up at Emily and feeling a strange warmth in her smile I laugh explaining that I am being "summoned."

"I hope that we might have the chance to speak again." I said feeling a little embarrassed. "We will." She confidently spoke still smiling.

I left to speak with the crowded group of old men and feeling worn after the day's activities, I excuse myself and walked towards the stairs. I couldn't help but look for the cream skirt as I walk out of the reception, but it is nowhere to be found. I retreat into bed recalling the night's festivities and the mysterious woman in the crowd. The aged Base 131 I have heard so much about since my arrival is the destination for the morning.

Turning the television on to help me fall asleep, I

flip to a late night British talk show. The host is talking about believing in strange phenomena and fate. "Do you believe in fate?" the host asks a famous guest sitting beside him, coffee cup in hand. "There are certain degrees of fate to believe in," he answers. "The question is really do you accept the fate you have chosen to believe?" Stumped by his answer, the host laughs and went to commercial. Just before closing my tired eyes I begin to think. How did those airmen accept their fate during the war? They never had a real choice, they just believed in fighting for the same thing...freedom. The word fate enters my mind once again and I wonder why my fate had lead me to England. "What is in store for me here?"

Chapter Four

The Return to Base 131

The next morning around 8:30 A.M., I sit on my
bed thinking about Joseph and bending over my suitcase
to take out an old letter. The edges are worn as if
someone had read it a thousand times and had made sure
it was perfect before sending. The ironic thing is that the
letter was never received; the stamp still gleamed in the
upper corner. My mind wandered to the contents of this
aged correspondence. The last time I had read the letter
was back in the dusty attic of my distant cousin's house
where it was discovered in the mysterious old suitcase. I
had been told by John Cosco, the bombardier of *Angel,*
that Joseph had met a women in England during the war
and the letter became a passionate remembrance of a love
that comforted two young people in a time of desperation.
Now, I unfold the creased letter and yearn to read it once
more. Now, it seems fitting, as I am close to where he
had met her, and I begin with the date scrawled in the

right corner; *July 17, 1944.* I remember the date of the tragic crash over Germany. The letter is only two days previous. It had probably been found among his things in England and sent back to his mother only to be kept locked away for five decades. Lost in thought for barely a moment, I return to reading the letter.

> *Dear Anne,*
>
> *I am missing you so much these days. I wonder how you are doing in London and what adventures you are getting into. London was so wonderful, much more exciting than the base. We are all in high spirits here. Our flight missions are becoming more frequent and our pilot, Dallas, is keeping us in line. There is so much I want to tell you. I recall the day we met and remind myself that there are good sides to being in a war. I envision your smile, your auburn hair tied back, and the*

navy Admiralty uniform that only you could look marvelous in. I was so nervous that day we met. I remember the kind smile you held for me as I saw you from across the hall at Rainbow Corner. I was awestruck by your sweetness and beauty. Then, you noticed me staring and laughed, sensing my apprehension. It was then that I knew I had to talk to you. Pretending to be the bold American soldier, I approached you, but in reality I was trembling with the nervousness of ten men. Those few days we spent together in London, reading in Hyde Park, and having endless conversation I will treasure always. My favorite place, though, is in Anstey at St. George's Church where we would sit silently praying for the end of the war to come. I hope that one day we may return to that same church and share our vows to each other. I never had the chance to tell you what an amazing person you truly are. No doubt you will be successful and I hope once the war has ended I can be a part of your life forever. I fell in love with you, Anne, that day you smiled at me and all the days in the weeks that followed. I have never felt this way about anyone before. Each mission I take, I pray that I will once again feel your embrace and smell the sweet scent of your hair. I fear that one day my final mission will come and I will not have had the chance to tell you everything I feel for you.

I pause, holding the letter and becoming more emotional with each word I read. It must have been such an emotional release for Joseph to write this to Anne. I can tell he truly cared for this woman whoever she may have been. I imagined Anne to be witty and funny complimenting his shy character. There was no picture of the two of them in the contents of the suitcase, so the only picture I knew was the stunning image I had in my head. Something compelled me to finish reading the letter. Joseph's scrawled handwriting covered almost two pages of the blue lined stationary. I continue to read:

> *I don't want you to worry about me. I will be fine. They are taking good care of us at the base and I hear good news everyday that the end of the war will be close. If something should happen, please know that I have loved you since I met you. You are my first love, Anne, and I hope that we will come again to Hyde Park and St. George's Church. I'll wear the locket you gave me as a symbol of how much you care for me. Well, I must go back to preparing for the next mission. You'll be happy to know I have been diligently playing my saxophone,*

as it seems to cheer up the men at the base.
I think we all need a little laughter around
here sometimes. I miss you terribly and hope
that this letter reaches you in good health.
I think of you always.

Love, Joseph

The ink towards the end of the letter is smeared and almost unreadable as if tears had fallen onto the paper smudging the words. I wonder how Anne would have felt if she had read the letter. After the first time I read the letter back in the attic, I wanted to know if Anne was still living. I wanted to give her the letter. I had wondered if she still felt this passion for my cousin even after all these years. After searching for weeks, I came across a Margaret Cruller who lived at Anne's street address. I called inquiring about Anne and discovered Mrs. Cruller had been an old friend of hers. Much to my disappointment, I then found out that Anne Howard had died of cancer in 1977. Now, she would never truly know the love Joseph had felt for her expressed in the letter. Deep down, I felt that she had known all along somehow even without the letter. She had to have known.

I mentioned Joseph's name and Margaret's voice became excited. She said that Anne spoke of Joseph quite often. "Anne had never married. She said that she could only love once and that love had been with Joseph," Margaret said solemnly. "She was so happy when they met and after his death she tried so hard to move on, but she couldn't bear to leave him behind. She wore a locket that was mysteriously returned to her until the day she died. She loved that locket. I remember when she went to the base and found out that he had been killed," her voice had trailed off.

"She was very religious and went to church regularly. She had the kindest heart and was always there to help," Margaret had said.

My conversation that night with Margaret helped me to know the woman my cousin had adored. Even after reading the letter for the second time, I wished with all my heart that it was possible to meet Anne and give the letter to her.

I carefully fold the letter and place it back into the cream envelope.

* * *

Promptly at 10:00 A.M. the group meets at the front lobby to load the buses for the short drive to Nuthampstead where a memorial service is to be held on the grounds of Base 131. I can tell from the sudden rush of the veterans to their seats that they are anxious to visit the sacred place. John Cosco sits beside of me and tells me how deeply Joseph's love for the saxophone affected the entire base. "The men of Base 131 would hear the sweet melodies coming from the plane hanger and know it was Joseph goofing around and making the others laugh and sing. He had a way of putting people at ease with his music." Cosco's face lit up as he spoke of my cousin.

One could tell that they had become close friends before the crash. The bus stops and I turn to look out the window seeing nothing I expected. There are wheat fields and grass growing high over the runways where majestic Flying Fortresses would have departed in 1944 and 1945. The control tower is no longer visible as it had been torn down to make use of the fields for farming. Near where the control tower once prominently stood, the Woodman Inn remains one of the last standing buildings at the base. Close to this Inn a flagpole and monument have been erected by "Friends of the 398th." The flagpole stands tall above the decaying buildings. I motion to John Cosco to follow me to the monument. It is up a slightly steep embankment and many of the veterans hesitate before taking the long strides needed to reach the top. A man in light blue trousers looking to be around eighty cautiously walks closer to the edge of the hill. His legs are weak and it appears that his knees would buckle at any moment causing him to collapse. I am already near the top of the embankment before I notice what this man is trying to do. His determination to reach the monument moves me. He, nodding away help or assistance, crouches down on his hands and knees and crawls up the embankment to the others. His dignity is far too great to accept help. He wishes to see the monument and not even his worn and tired body can prevent him from victory. I turn to John and ask who this determined man is. "That's Bob Hart, he was a co-pilot of the 600th squadron and is a fine man." I want to talk to this man who I now feel honored to hold company with. I walk timidly towards this old hero who stands at the base of the monument his cheeks stained with tears. No doubt he is remembering his crew, his friends, and the tortured moments of fear while fighting in combat. I am wondering how I can casually interrupt his thoughts but I didn't have to wonder long, he interrupts mine.

"Son, do you know what it is like to lose someone? To be helpless and afraid and at moments your entire life flashes before your eyes? I knew then and sometimes can still feel it now," his voice is shaky and his lips quiver as he speaks. Others from the tour start to gather closer around the monument for a prepared short commemoration service.

"No sir, I don't think I have known that feeling yet," I answer. Although I was only eighteen years younger than this man, I feel like a child who is a little intimidated by a brave war hero.

"That is why I came here to this place, that is why I had to make it to the monument for the service. I need to put some of those frightening feelings of despair and loss behind me. After fifty-five years I am ready to let my crew go, to let my friends go, and to commemorate them and myself for what we did back then for you today."

I am moved as he speaks and remember how these men standing here today defended our honor and freedom. Who knows what the country would be like today if they hadn't fought and won the freedom that is taken for granted each day.

People begin to encircle the monument and an opening hymn is sung by an older woman wearing a pink and yellow flowered sun dress. She and her dress stand out in the sea of people as her high pitched voice rings clearly and soars through the clouds. An American flag is lowered at the flagpole and the group respectfully remains silent for two minutes of prayer and thought. Silence is broken as Wally Blackwell raises the flag, and proudly says,

> *"They shall not grow old; Age shall not weary them, nor the years condemn. At the going down of the sun, and in the morning, we will remember them."*

The group pauses for reflection; deep sobs are heard as people bow their heads. The hymn *How Great Thou Art* is heard coming from the familiar high pitched voice in the back of the crowd as slowly others join in.

Soon everyone is on the brink of tears as people remember their loved ones and the lives they abruptly lost. The Reverend Gerald Drew, Rector of Anstey, Brent Pelham, Meesden, Great and Little Hormead, and Wyddial recites a prayer and later he says in a solemn and reflective voice...

> *"Let us remember before God, and commend to His safe keeping: Those who have died for their country in war; Those whom we knew and whose memory we treasure; All those who have lived and died in the service of mankind."*

As the roll of honour is read, I stand listening to the names of the two hundred ninety-two men who gave their lives during the war torn years of 1944 and 1945. My thoughts are broken by a verse that the Reverend Drew recited just moments earlier...

> *"Those whom we knew and whose memory we treasure."*

Now it was my turn to feel the soft tears caress my

face.

"Joseph Doglio," Wally Blackwell reads my cousins name as the reading of the two hundred ninety-two souls continued. "I'm here Joseph, I'm here," I say this to no one in particular and yet I am confident that Joseph hears me. Almost whispering, I say it again. "I'm here." The tears continue to dampen my face. I am unashamed and I can only wonder what emotions Joseph's parents suffered when they were told of their son's death. "Oh, dear God how does a parent endure the loss of a child...."

Children, ages seven through ten, move toward the hill and carefully place bouquets of flowers at the base of the monument. Even they show respect as they slowly move away, their heads bowed, in childlike reverence.

There are a few more hymns before Father Michael Roberts of St. Richard's Catholic Church in Buntingford offers a moving prayer. I wonder where these men, The Reverend Drew and Father Roberts find these adequate words for a day such as this.

The closing hymn is appropriately the serenely haunting *Amazing Grace*. Everyone remains standing until the last verse is sung. A uniformed Honor Guard ceremonially salutes the flag and the group begins to walk slowly in a five minute procession from the monument to the Woodman Inn. The restaurant and Inn has a square thatched roof with a weathered shingled front. A curtained window rested above the framed wooden sign reading in faded white letters "The Woodman Inn where all your journeys end." The pub is something of a local landmark as it has been standing in Nuthampstead for almost four hundred years. The owners traditionally greet the group as we enter the charming restaurant. They tell us a brief history of the pub making reference to the soldiers of Base 131 frequenting the casual atmosphere of the place. I notice an open fire near the bar which appears to be well used yet taken care of by its owners. The restaurant is crowded with smiling people laughing and talking with their glasses of ale. The veterans in the group move towards the bar each confidently ordering a Guinness. I had heard earlier from John Cosco that this is the famous drink of the veterans of Base 131. I reach the bar starting to converse with Ed Soule and he coaxes me into trying my first Guinness. Never having an acquired taste for beer, I hesitated at first, but to avoid being rude, I gratefully take the glass. Bob Hart, John Cosco and around half-a-dozen other veterans jovially join in a toast made by Ed Soule.

"I am so glad we could come together again in England. I remember when I first was sent here. I was scared, unknowing of the dangers and horrors of war." His voice became shaky and low as he continued, "I remember seeing the town and the first time I came here to Base 131. I recall thinking that if I were shot down on my first, last or any mission in between, there would be nothing in life I would have missed. This place came to mean so much to me. So, I toast what remains of Base

131 and what remains of those memories of B-17's, friends, and dignity. To the members of the 398th, may we all live on to remember we have missed nothing in life." The men reminisce for almost an hour and then collectively decide to return to the hotel to rest before dinner. Since the rest of the day and night is set aside as free, I decide to stay at the Woodman a little longer.

I notice an old man sitting alone in a dark wooden booth. His Guinness rests on the side of the table and a scornful look blanketed his aged face. I casually stroll by the booth still wearing my name tag and notice he has one pinned to his white oxford shirt. I decide to pause at the booth asking if he would mind some company. He looks up from his glass, his eyes sad and weary and half smiles. I slide into the booth and grab the attention of the waiter requesting a cup of tea. He takes a sip of his Guinness and looking up at me says, "Sonny, you can't come to the Woodman and order a tea. You have to try a Guinness, its tradition began by me and the other airmen stationed here." I smiled explaining that I had already experienced a Guinness with the other veterans and laughing I thanked him for his concern. I stare at the features of the old man sitting before me. His hair is gray and thinning and he has it combed to one side. His eyes, dark brown in color, are alert and sharp as he talks. He has several discolored age spots on his forehead and cheeks that intermingle with the puzzle of lines and crevices on his face. He introduces himself as Mr. Allen Sutton, a pilot of the 602nd squadron. The waiter, to the disappointment of Allen, brings the hot tea. He decides to order another Guinness. I watch the old mans hand as he lifts the glass of the brown ale. His hand is shaking so much that he spills a bit of foam down the side of his goblet. The hand holding the glass is full of lines and one knuckle is slightly swollen, perhaps broken from an accident years ago. I cannot resist studying him as he continues to talk about the adventures of Base 131. As he lifts the glass again, I look at his other hand, yet to my surprise there is no hand, only an empty sleeve. I didn't noticed the handicap until now. I resist the urge to question him about the missing hand and instead casually ask about the ale.

"So, do you enjoy the ale? Did you come here a lot during the war?"

He doesn't answer. He blankly stares out the window. I can't pinpoint exactly what he is looking at, but something tells me it is unimportant to know. I remain silent and I do not want to interrupt his thoughts.

The old man looks down into his glass of ale, as if it were a wishing well, his hand is trembling. "Yes," he says out of nowhere, "we came here at the end of almost everyday. This pub became a place to meet friends and to laugh. Each night for some, it was the last time that they would experience any bit of fun."

He pauses for what seems like an eternity. "I lost so many friends, Sonny." Slowly, a tear makes its way to a crease under his eye. The tear moves along the crease and begins a long journey down his cheek. Finally, after making its way through a maze of lines it reaches the edge of his lip. He brushes it away with his sleeve. The empty sleeve.

"Your friends, Sir?" The humorous moments have passed and I become solemn. Words are hard to find and the conversation seems to have slowed to a halt. I know what he is thinking but having the utmost respect and admiration for this old man, I wait before saying anything else.

The old man takes another drink, savoring the taste. From the pockets of brown pants he removes a limp handkerchief. I can't help but notice that his shirt is tattered and soiled. Several stains are visible near the front pocket. One button is hanging on by a thin thread. He moves the soiled handkerchief across his face and then he returns it to his pocket.

"Friends, laddie," he softly whispers. I notice I am no longer called Sonny.

Gathering my thoughts I sincerely ask the old man, "Would you like to talk about them Sir?"

The old man briskly shakes his head, "No," he answers. "I keep it to myself. No use tormenting other folks with my demons."

"If I may be so bold to say, perhaps there are times when it's good to talk about memories." Then I add, "Good memories and," putting an emphasis on the word and, "and bad memories."

"Not these, Sonny." I'm Sonny again.

"Well, I won't continue to pry, but if you ever feel like talking this week, I'm willing to listen." I reach over to shake his hand and realize, somewhat embarrassed, that I have my hand suspended in midair. He looks at me and then at his empty sleeve.

"You're not the first. Many people have done that before. Don't be so dadburned embarrassed," he said smiling.

I now feel comfortable enough to ask. "How did it

happen?"

Another drink of ale. "A long time ago. 1945. Over Munich."

"Flak or fighter plane?" I curiously ask.

The old man looks toward the street. The late afternoon sun is beginning to set casting an orange glow on the trees. Turning his gaze from the street towards me, his voice cracking, he begins.

"The target was a saturation bombing of Munich. The flight went smoothly as we crossed into France and then Germany." He paused for a drink of ale before continuing. "As we approached the IP I stretched my legs out past the rudder peddle and was flexing my shoulders, arms, and neck trying to relax. As I reached down to grasp the controls I noticed a single German aircraft had broken through our formation. He came from nowhere." His voice seemed to tighten as if the event was happening again, not fifty-five years ago, but at this very moment. "Damn bloodsucker!"

"We felt a sudden and high shrilled thump. The bombardier section disengaged from the fortress. One of our props cut down through the cockpit, maybe eight to twelve inches aft of the top line of the windscreen. The controls became mushy. Our aircraft was falling off, nose down," his voice was shaking and his hand was trembling as he held onto his glass of ale.

"My co-pilot and I somehow got control of the plane and miraculously we made it back to base." His gaze turned back to the orange glow that painted the trees. There were several moments of silence. "Oh," he hesitated, "we landed ole Nellie. The ambulances, fire trucks and medics came along," tears again filled his eyes. "I lost my hand but my bombardier and navigator lost much more. I'd give everything if I could have them back."

We sit in silence for a few minutes. Voices begin to fill the room. Local college students are making their way to the bar for a pint and some relaxation. The old man looks around. He, like myself, is examining the faces of young men and women. They pass our booth smiling, laughing, full of energy and spirit.

"I'm an old man, Sonny. But once I was young like them." His voice is louder as he shoots a finger toward a gathering table a few feet away. "I was strong and fought a war and watched as my friends gave their lives for freedom," his voice begins to rise to become even louder. "I did what I did because I believed in America and I believed in England. I believed in the people." Then with emotion choking his voice, "And my friends. I believed in my friends." Another tear made its way down his face, but this tear lingered. I felt a surge of emotion and compassion.

"Now that I'm old, nobody remembers. Nobody." He frustratingly slaps his hand on the table. His ale totters but does not spill.

The room had become silent. The young students were looking towards us. Not just the students near our booth but all the students. I wonder what's going through their minds as they listen to this emotional old man.

"I remember sir," I stammer, "that's why I am here. Here in Cambridge, Nuthampstead, and tomorrow to Anstey. I'm here to remember you, my cousin, and his crew. I haven't forgotten, Sir, I never have. I never will."

Looking at him I can see his pain. Or is it loneliness. Maybe it's both. I thought, have we, the younger generations disappointed him? Have we not said thank you enough to those who fought for us? I finally begin to understand. He sacrificed his youth back then to fly heavy bombers, lose his arm, and watch his friends die all for the freedom and happiness of future generations to come.

"I'm sorry," he says, removing his soiled handkerchief one more time. "I'm feeling a bit of despair. Just being here brings back all the ghosts that I could never escape from my mind."

"Don't be sorry." My mouth opens yet no words come out. I glance at the room and notice the students still staring in silence as if we are a movie in process.

"Let's go now," the old man says in a low whisper.

"Sure, we should go back to the hotel. Can I help you?"

Before I can stand to reach for his wrinkled hand, a young man approaches our booth. He extends his hand to aged warrior. A look of surprise crosses the old mans face.

"Why, thank you young man. That's very kind of you," he says in a soft voice.

"No Sir, not at all Sir," the young man replies politely.

Suddenly and surprisingly, one by one, the students stand. They move forward from their chairs. They form a staggered line from our booth to the door. As we pass, some extended their hands shaking the old man's weathered hand. They wanted to witness the hero and express their gratitude in the best way they knew how.

As we reach the door, the young man who has helped my friend from the booth once again extends his hand. The lad is a giant of a man. Probably twenty years of age, broad shoulders and at least six feet five inches tall.

He looks at the old man. For a brief moment they stand together until the silence is broken by the young student from Peterhouse College.

"We haven't forgotten, Sir. My grandfather served in the war. He was lost at sea." The boy is sincere and he smiles at my new friend.

The old man returns the smile, his eyes sparkling with pride. A young woman in the crowd of students begins a soft applause. The applause grows louder as other join in and the smile on the old mans face grows larger and larger. A tear once again forms in the corner of his eye. This tear is a tear of joy.

For one brief moment I feel as though he, in his

mind, was in the air again. His cherished B-17 was airborne. The applause was the engines and the cheers became the wind, passing the waist gunners opening.

"Let's go Sonny, we need to get back to the hotel." He salutes the crowd still grinning and turns to the door.

To the giant young man standing beside me I say, "You just saved an old man from despair. I honestly believe you renewed his hope. Thank you." I look with admiration at this youthful giant.

He grinned and replied, "Not to worry, Sir. We won't forget. Tell him again, for all of us."

"I will, thank you," I replied shocked at the maturity in his actions.

"On your way then." He points outside. "He's moving on without you."

"You're right. I'm leaving now."

I closed the door behind me, looked ahead to the old man and then back at the door.

"He called me Sir," I say out loud smiling.

I begin to run trying to catch him but he had walked at a rather brisk pace for an older man. Finally catching him I say, "Hey wait up."

"What's the matter, Sonny, can't keep up with us old folks?" His spirit has returned and he turns fiesty.

Winded and laughing I answered, "No Sir, I really can't. Don't think I'll try today."

"Good," he boldly proclaimed. "Won't do you any good."

"Yes, Sir."

Then he did a half step, kicked up a heel and pointed at me. "By willies, I'm feeling chipper today."

I watched him walk ahead of me. I looked to heaven continuing to walk down the road and smiling said aloud, "Thank you God, for the wonders of old people." I took two more steps watching him nearing the main road, "and God, for young people as well."

Chapter Five

The Church Service

Feeling emotionally overwhelmed from the memorial service at Base 131 and the encounter with Allen Sutton, I decide to rest for the night. After a quick dinner in the downstairs of the hotel, I grab the John Grisham book I had not finished on the plane and sit in my room reading until I can fall asleep.

The next morning, the sunlight streams through the windows and onto my face. I think how ironic it is to be woken up in that manner because it has not been too sunny since we arrived in England. I grumble a little, wanting to stay in bed a bit longer, yet I know that today is the biggest event of the trip. It is the dedication of the memorial window at the St. George's Church in Anstey. I will finally be able to see the remarkable stained glass window that everyone had been speaking of. I shower, dress in a dark blue suit and a red tie and walk to meet the others in the lobby. On the way to the lobby, I grab a croissant and a cup of moderately warm coffee bumping into Allen Sutton. He is dressed in a black suit, his shirt a little wrinkled and his tie in an incomplete knot. I can tell by his mismatched socks that his wife, now at home, had usually been the one to dress him each day. He greets me with a firm handshake from his able hand and asks if I am excited to see the window.

"None of us have seen it yet. It is suppose to be a sight, I hear." He mutters while pouring a glass of orange juice from the continental breakfast table.

"Yes, I am anxious to see the unveiling," I say. "My cousins name is etched on it along with the other two hundred ninety-two names and I hope that I will, in a way, be saluting him for his bravery by being there."

"He'll know you are there," he stammers while buttering a piece of toast. "He'll know."

We walk briskly towards the lobby as I notice people beginning to load the bus. Everyone is dressed in more formal clothing than the previous tours. People seem to be anxious to see the window, but a little intimidated about visiting the old church. John Cosco tells me on the bus ride that the church has existed since the late 12th century. It has been rebuilt infinite times since then, yet parts of the present church can be dated to the times of William the Conqueror. He tells me that the soil in which the church rests is not only historical but sacred as well. Romans and Saxons had tread and built on the land forming the walls that housed the first Christians. I can only sit in awe as I am being told of the age and history of the structure I am about to visit.

The bus pulls close to the brick wall which separates the English lane from the churchyard. The church itself is made of white and gray stone and patches of mortar. The entrance is an oval doorway coming to a point at the top. Two smaller windows rest on either side of the doorway as one enormous bullet shaped window peaks above the door. A bell tower stands almost directly in the middle of the church with diagonal buttresses up to the very top where a small spike rests. I am gazing in amazement, as is the entire group, at the ancient and mystical looking church. Woods surround the grounds and I am told there are trails leading to peaceful resting places. I wonder how many people throughout the ages have stopped to pray at the church or to seek comfort within its walls.

As I am walking into the front entrance, someone calls my name from the back of the crowd. John, politely pushing through the group, reaches me and tells me that he has remembered something about my cousin.

"Seeing this church has flooded my mind with memories. This is where Joseph would come with Anne to pray. I remember him talking about it and although I had been here only once, I remember this pathway, a distinct trail he would joke about called Pains End. He would say that this is where he could come to ease his personal sorrows." He then points to my left at a worn rectangular wooden sign in which burned letters read, "Pains End..."

"This is where he would come, to find his peace,"

he continues. "We all had our places to go. For some it was the pubs, for others the streets of town, but for Joseph it was here." The procession into the church is slowing as people are now shoulder to shoulder squeezing through the doorway.

I am startled for a moment. I begin running through my mind all of the places we had visited through the week and Joseph had been to most, yet it is here that he truly had wanted to be. A place where he never felt afraid. An old, sacred church whose pews I notice, as I enter, are faded and scratched and the walls are covered in etchings of shields and English crests from centuries earlier. Gothic style arches hold up the stone structure and are topped with the moldings of carved mythical creatures in marble. The font, I learn, dates back to Norman Times. It has been in use for nearly one thousand years. I notice the nave arcades which perhaps illustrate a rather uncertain transition from Norman Times to the early English style. Amongst the graffiti on the walls I can't help but notice many invocations of the Virgin

Mary. Seeing those invocations remind me of my childhood in South Wilmington, Illinois. I begin to smile as I recall being the only protestant boy in our small prairie town. Despite my protestant roots, everything I did, seemed to be done with Catholics.

I was taken by the choir stalls which surely dated back to the 17th century. I am in awe of this holy place. I sit in silence as my eyes search every corner for more history. I wonder if I will sit any where close to where Joseph sat with Anne. The very thought intrigues me.

A red cloth is draped over the memorial window and people begin to quietly sit in the pews facing the alter. The alter is small with an undetermined style. It too must date back hundreds of years. My eyes focus on an ancient chest sitting near the organ. Later I learn that the ironbound box dates to 1597. I sit next to John Cosco and his wife in the second pew from the front. I am a little nervous sitting so close to the alter, but I am relieved after people begin to sit around me. A soft melody is heard coming from the back of the church and a choir of veterans begin to sing. Six bells in the tower chime in the background of the choir for almost twenty minutes before the service begins. Whispers can be heard across the aisle as veterans and families point and admire the ornamentation and beauty of the church. Everyone rises as the processional hymn, *For All the Saints* rings through the voices of the congregation. John leans over whispering that Lord Bishop of St. Albans is to perform the dedication and His Royal Highness the Duke of Gloucester is to unveil the window. The congregation sits, as we are welcomed to the hallowed church for this ceremonial and moving occasion. A verse from Isaiah is read by the Duke of Gloucester. He reads the ten verses of Isaiah, Chapter 35. His voice is strong and it echoes through the one thousand year old church. It is as though he is raising the spirits of the men who have gone before. His words resound through the air and when he is finished I am truly fed by the words of an old testament prophet. I am suddenly aware that some unknown experience awaits me. I can feel it.

A sob is heard from behind me as *America the Beautiful* echoes through the raised ceilings of the church. I turn to wipe a tear on my sleeve and am offered a handkerchief by John's wife. I graciously take the white linen cloth and dab my eyes. The emotion flooding the church is not only affecting me, a visitor and friend, but is beginning to reach those veterans around me. As prayers for humility, peace, and boldness are spoken by the Bishop, I see those men, once young and brave soldiers, weeping into the shoulders and handkerchiefs of those sitting beside them. A message from James Duvall, the chaplain of the 398th Bomb Group is read by Allen Ostrom, a veteran of the 603nd squadron. Duvall had not lived to see the window dedication as he passed only months earlier. His words rang clearly this day and it is to some as though he is still there, helping the airmen through prayer and hope as he had fifty-six years ago.

"Today we living members of
the 398th Bomb Group, lift high
the flaming torch of freedom

passed to us by our comrades whose lives were given in battle against totalitarianism. We remember those lives that never had the opportunity to grow old with us. They gave their lives that others could live free. Many never had the opportunity to experience the youthful years of life, grow into manhood, have a family, and enjoy the golden years. We have all benefitted from the gift of their supreme sacrifice. Today we stand in humility and gratitude. We are thankful that we were able to share a bit of life with all those names inscribed on the memorial window. We may forget what has been said here, but never let us forget what was done here. May the God of all men keep and bless you."

A muffled cry is heard as a veteran remembers the good chaplain.

Following the Lord's Prayer and another hymn, the unveiling begins with a few words from His Royal Highness.

The red curtain is carefully removed and sunlight pushes through the brightly colored glass making it a clear and magnificent sight. Three tall, narrow, and rectangular windows comprise the memorial. The tops of the windows appear to be scalloped in a three-leaf clover shape. The first window intertwines B-17, Flying Fortresses with brilliantly colored butterflies in a pillar of smoke including a brilliantly white dove at the top. Deep greens and shades of blue adorn the first window. In the mass of clouds, on this window, are B-17 Flying Fortresses flying upward to the sky and identified with the

398th by having a triangle "W" on the tail. I learn, through the dedication, that the pillar of smoke in the first window symbolizes what led the Israelites by day. The same aircraft are visible on the third window descending in downward spiral flames of fire which symbolize what led the Israelites by night. Clearly, the third window is a disturbing depiction of the anguish and violence of World War II. The center window is a peaceful median with dozens of brightly colored orange, blue, and yellow butterflies floating up into the top of the window. Some of the butterflies have the imprints of numbers and logos of the four squadrons stationed at Base 131. The bishop then acknowledges the two hundred ninety-two names etched in tiny letters on the window. I tune his voice out thinking about finding my own cousin's name on the window. The names are a formal recognition and commemoration of their bravery and are to remain forever in the church.

A minute of silence by the congregation follows the dedication. The blowing of noses and the cries of people scattered in the pews break the silence. The Bishop prepares the blessing and the choir quietly starts *Glory Glory Hallelujah*. The singing gets louder and louder as more people join in putting away their handkerchiefs. After the hymn is finished the national anthems of both the United States and the United Kingdom ring from the standing congregation. The anthems solidify our union. Two great Nations continuing to be bound together by a common purpose. Then the church rector leads the congregation in one final Act of Remembrance.

"Let us remember before God, and commend to his safe keeping: Those who have died for their country in war; Those whom we knew, and whose memory we treasure; All those who have lived and died in the service of mankind." He continues, asking the congregation to repeat...

> *"They shall not grow old, As*
> *we that are left grow old; At*
> *the going down of the sun and*
> *in the morning we will*

remember them. "

The final song surprises me yet not a dry eye is visible in the entire church as it is played. The organist plays *Dixie.*

It is a song which has come to mean to Americans a prevailing over the shortcomings that have been endured through the years.

Dixie brings deep emotions to many people in America. Some would like to destroy it's music and words while others would want it's stirring melody to be remembered forever.

On this day, it is played beautifully by an organist who feels a passion for music and not for a cause. To me, at that moment, *Dixie* fires my passions. It is not only me who is affected by its melody but an entire church seems to unleash it's emotions.

"Old times there are not forgotten."

As I listen, one word comes to my mind. I can't seem to remove it from my thoughts. Perhaps if we would somehow embrace the meaning of this single word we would, in some small way, find a cornerstone to build upon. A strong and inspiring cornerstone built on *TOLERANCE*.

The service ends as ushers lead the rows of pews to the back of the church. The bells chime again as the procession of people exit the church with their heads bowed down and walking slower than when they came in.

Chapter Six

Joseph's Legacy

Lunch at the High Hill Farm in Anstey is scheduled after the service and although I didn't have the appetite for any sort of food, I follow the group to sit at white clothed tables set up outside in the sunshine. Each table has a different colored vase holding bunches of summer wild flowers and providing a sweet lingering scent in the air. I notice the vase at my table is a crystalline blue the color of a Carolina blue sky back home.

The lunch is arranged buffet style with an assortment of finger sandwiches, fresh fruit and tasty looking salads. I walk up to the long rectangular buffet table putting a spoonful of potato salad and a small cucumber sandwich on my plate and return to my table. Not thinking anything of the small amount of food I put on my plate John Cosco and Ed Soule laugh jokingly, asking if I had enough food to eat. I smile telling them

I truly wasn't hungry at the moment but was sure in a few hours that I would be famished again. The farm is a beautiful spread of land and is as green as the rolling hills I had seen earlier on the trip. Excusing myself from the table, I walk the grounds in a daze admiring the view and thanking the occasional breezes that cooled the heat from the blazing sun. I suddenly feel a hand on my shoulder and turn to find myself face to face with the beautiful woman from the reception at the hotel. She wasn't wearing a cream skirt this time, yet the grey pants she wore were flattering and her smile eased my nervousness and surprise to see her again.

"I didn't think I would see you again this trip," I stammer. There is something very familiar about her, yet I couldn't put my finger on what it is. "Where have you been? I haven't seen you with the tour; you seemed to have disappeared."

"Oh," she blushes. "I guess I am not as noticeable as I sometimes think I am. I'm just a rather plain, ordinary person. Not one to stand out in a crowd," she giggled.

"That may be your opinion, but you certainly made a lasting first impression on me. I find it difficult to put this into words but sometimes I feel as though we have known each other for years." I feel a little embarrassed, yet I am completely comfortable talking to her.

She laughs as she waves Allen Sutton over and into our conversation.

"Do you know Allen?" I ask, because I had just met this new friend at the Woodman Inn yesterday.

"Oh, we only just met today," she says moving closer to my side. "He was telling me about his time in London during the war, and about his accident."

"Yes, I came to discover myself what a brave man he is." I confidently say. "I'm sure he has some great stories. London must hold fond memories for all the veterans."

Her mind seems to drift for a brief moment as her eyes shift from my face and focus on a green spread in the distance. She surprises me with her next comment. "Oh London was a wonderful place during the war. We had the blitz and all, but one can never forget those priceless moments shared by desperate people seeking refuge from those terrible fears of war. It was then that London was alive with emotion and love." Her voice quivers for a moment before she regains composure.

A curious grin crossed my face. This woman does not look old enough to have lived and remember the war years, yet she recalls them as clearly as if 1944 was only yesterday. I couldn't help but question her. "You speak of these times as if you remember them." My eye catches a glimpse of a small tear welling in her left eye. "Did you have a relative recall them to you?"

She didn't answer. The silence makes the moment between us awkward. It is then that Allen, after being distracted and detained by other groups of people, makes his way over to us.

"Hi, it is a beautiful day here in Anstey, don't you agree?" His cheerfulness interrupted the silence.

"Yes, it is nice weather," I nod and notice her nodding in agreement with me.

Allen becomes engrossed in conversation with a passing stranger and I turn to her again. "Are you okay?" I still feel uneasy. I knew I had pried into a memory that was painfully deep within her heart.

"What?" she turns to face me again. "Oh sorry, yes, I am fine," she spoke softly. "I'm quite alright, it's just the girl in me that becomes emotional sometimes. There are times that I think about being a young girl alive with the wonderful moments and memories of a time long ago that was so meaningful to me." She smiles again and my heart is relieved that she hadn't been upset at anything I had said. Looking a little uneasy, she fingers a tiny gold chain around her neck. I notice at the end of the chain swung an oval locket which she twisted nervously as she spoke. The locket appears old, the gold dull in color and the clasp bent. It looks as if it is something she had not taken off in years.

"That's a lovely necklace," I say inquisitively. I wondered if her family or her husband had given it to her. I am curious to know if pictures of them were hidden inside.

She smiles blushing, and embarrassed removes her hands from the locket.

"Thank you, it's priceless." Her smile becomes mischievous. "Maybe one day you will give a locket to Kathryn or your daughter Andrea. Women treasure old jewelry."

Baffled, I wonder how she knows my wife and daughter's names. I hadn't told her. Who had?

"Wait," I jokingly say. "How do you know my wife and daughters names?"

Repeating my laugh she says, "I have my ways."

"No, really," I plead still grinning. "Whom have

you been talking to about me?"

"Well, lets just say a member of the 398th.." She turns to face the tables outside and catches the eye of Allen bringing him over to our conversation again.

"Let's all go for a drive," she says looking at Allen and me. "I have some things to show you that you might both enjoy."

The next thing I know we are driving in her car down an English lane. The afternoon is free for the tour group, so I think nothing of leaving the others to do some exploring with this intriguing woman. Allen is excited to visit the other sites with a woman who seems to know everything about England already, and I am glad to be in both of their company once more.

We drive in silence for several minutes and finally I blurt out, "Where are you taking us?"

"To see, hear, and feel things you could never experience on tours. This is the unofficial tour of Anstey and Cambridge, my dear," she giggled and kept her eyes intent on the road.

For the remainder of the puzzling drive we speak very little. Occasionally, a word is muttered in awe of the countryside by Allen or me and then the silence would creep into the car again. I stare at her during the drive noticing the sparkle in her blue eyes and the light streaks in her brown hair. She looks to be a young woman, yet I dare not ask her age. I know women get offended easily when men question age and appearance. She is a charming and eloquent person to talk with. When she speaks, she has a lovely English accent and often classic words such as "chum" and "swell" escape her lips making me laugh.

She pulls the car over to the side of the lane, the wheels treading through the tall grass and asks us to step out for a moment. My shiny black shoes are moistened by the grass. What I see was breathtaking. We were looking out at the airstrip of Base 131. We aren't where we had been touring yesterday. Instead, the old runway, at this angle, looks longer, more magnificent; I could almost picture the majestic old planes soaring into the sky. I realize we were back in Nuthampstead. Allen jokes around telling us how he used to spend time when not in combat, chewing on wheat, looking at the sky and remembering home in Iowa. He chuckles remembering how the other crew members would call him the little country boy and imitate his accent.

"It was ironic, though," he said looking at Emily. "Because we were all little country boys, at least most of us. We all wanted to go home to the wheatfields and diners of our youth. We just had to laugh and hope each day that we would get to come home."

Emily smiles at Allen and for a minute I can tell in her eyes that she understands him. She sees and knows how he and the others had felt and dreamed back then.

"Let's take a walk, shall we?" She leads us from the car and down a small hill to an old path said to have been made by the Romans. At the end of the path, is a hollow, a slight dip in the terrain. She suddenly stops, informing us that this is where the men of the 602nd were quartered. The 602nd was Joseph's group. I try to picture in my mind the base and what it must have been like in 1944. As if she had read my thoughts she says, "It was a busy place, planes departing, loud engines and people bustling nonstop in the control towers. I don't think there ever was a moment of peace here." I want to question whom, she had known who had experienced the base, but I hold back admiring the scenery.

She then leads us further down the path, Allen and I following closely behind.

"This path was once a Roman road," she proclaims. "It wove its way through England and during the war it served as a footpath for the 602nd members." The path widens and we are now at the foot of the base runway. It is barely visible, just two skid lines in the grass, yet I can tell it had been the essence of the base at one time.

"Just stand here for a minute and be really quiet," her voice coming to a low whisper. Allen and I give each other puzzling looks and shrugging my shoulders I obey her request. A few seconds pass as I stare down the runway, my thoughts running through my head of who this woman is.

And then it came.

A sudden gust of wind brushes my face, its coolness giving me slight goose bumps on my arms and neck. A sound, deep, guttural can be heard in the distance becoming louder as if it is approaching the three of us. At first I thought I was crazy hearing things until I looked over at Allen standing beside me looking intensely at the runway, his arm hairs standing straight up, his mouth open. I look over at Emily wondering if she is hearing anything and she stands still, one hand clasping her locket the other resting at her side. I turn and continue to look forward, afraid at what I am hearing and what is approaching, yet my feet are unable to move, planted in the tall grass. My legs are cement blocks heavy with fear. The sound grew closer before I realize what it is. After thirty years of watching old Jimmy Stewart war movies, the sound is familiar. It is the distinct sound of huge steel engines coasting through the sky. Possibly, B-17 Flying Fortresses taking off and returning from missions. I feel as though my imagination is running wild, but after two minutes of deafening grumbling, the noise stops and the wind disappears. I turn to the other two people and stammer, "Did you hear that?"

Allen with his mouth still agape, eyes wide with curiosity replies, "That was the strangest wind I have ever heard. England does have some peculiar weather."

I looked at Allen not believing it was the wind, the color, I knew, had drained from my face.

Emily laughs dropping the locket against her chest. "There is another place here I would like to take you, but we need to drive to it."

We walk up the hill to the car. I lag behind repeatedly glancing behind me at the runway as if expecting the arrival of a Flying Fortress at any minute.

On the road, Emily reaches into her purse, pulls out a cell phone and dials a number. Thinking she is calling home or work, I excuse the call until to Allen and my surprise she hands the phone to Allen sitting peacefully in the back seat.

"I think you want to talk to someone. I think she needs to talk to you." She says while handing him the phone.

Allen took the small phone and gasps hearing the voice on the other end.

"Joanna?" His eighty-year-old brow crinkles surprised at who it is. "It's me honey, How are you feeling? Have you been following the doctor's orders? I miss you. Yes, Cambridge is wonderful. I've met the most amazing people here." His voice chokes as tears well into his eyes. "Don't worry about me honey, I'm fine... I think about you every minute." He pauses wiping his sleeve on his streaked face. "I'll see you when I come home in a few days, I love you." He hangs up the phone and handed it back to Emily who is still driving.

"How do you know my wife?' he asks sniffling.

"I just knew you wanted to talk to her. How is she doing?"

"Much better," he replies. I notice she has done a good job changing the subject, but I still wonder how she knows his wife is ill and more over, how she knows the number to call? The car stops and I realize we are back at St. George's Church in Anstey.

"There is something here I would like to share with you," she says.

Allen, still emotional from speaking to his wife, looks at us as we climb out of the car. "I think I might stay in the car, my legs are a little tired. You two go on ahead for a while."

"Are you sure you don't mind," I ask wanting to go with Emily but feeling bad leaving my friend behind.

"I'm sure, Sonny. I'm not as athletic as I used to be," he grins.

Feeling strange from the occurrence on the runway and thinking about the phone call in the car, I cautiously followed her. I put the mysterious sound in the back of my mind dismissing it as what Allen suggested is "wind", yet I still can't figure out how she knows about Allen's wife. Sighing, I look up to see the familiar sign "Pains End." This morning I had wanted to venture down the path to find where it led, but hadn't had the time after the service. After walking I discover that the path wraps around the church and then past the church yard cemetery and into a green wooded area.

She quickens her pace coming to a large oak tree a distance from the church. I am out of breath while attempting to catch up with her and she notices my exhaustion and suggests we take a rest under the shade of the enormous oak tree.

There is something unusual about this woman. She is outgoing and pleasant, yet there is a secret in her eyes. As we sit for a moment under the tree, we didn't say a word. The events of the day run wild in my mind. By placing her hand on top of mine, Emily dissolves the questions in my head, leaving me in peace and at ease. I look at her, the warmth coming from her smile, and experiencing a feeling that I had known her before.

"Why don't you take a picture here? Someday you will find it most meaningful to you."

"Can I take it with you?" I ask hoping I can have some remembrance of this woman.

"No, I'm afraid I'm not too photogenic; I don't take pictures too well," she blushes.

I take her advice, and using my camera, take a picture of the tree and the panoramic view of the church grounds. She is looking out past the tree and back at the path when the flash of the camera startles her.

"Excuse me," I say jokingly. "I didn't mean to get you in the picture."

She smiles. "I'm just warning you that I take a terrible picture."

I hear the film rewind as the roll is finished. Taking the film out, I put it in my pocket and place the camera in its case. I return to sitting next to her.

"I thought you would enjoy your time here. It's a special place."

"Yes, I do. I feel like some kind of emotional release has come over me. It's hard to explain..." I sheepishly trail off.

"I understand, I sometimes have that feeling here."

"When I was younger I used to come here with a friend. . . to feel peace," she glows at that moment, her skin a luminescent white. She touches the locket with her fingers.

"I love the beauty and tranquility of the old

church. Let's go sit in the church, shall we?" She begins to stand up brushing the grass from her pants and stretching her arms.

I want to do whatever she wishes, and I follow her lead up the path symbolically called "Pains End" and to the doorway of the church. It has cleared out since the service. Most people went to eat lunch or to explore Anstey on their own. It is quiet in the chapel. Only the crackle of lit candles set beside the alter interruptes the peace.

I walk behind her to the second pew, amazingly the same one I had sat in hours earlier, and we move sitting in the middle facing the alter. She kneels, softly saying a prayer to herself.

"This church holds memories for me," she whispers. "And now it has that beautiful stained glass window making it even more meaningful and special to me."

Walking to the window, Emily waves me over.

"Is this what you are looking for?" Puzzled I focus on what her finger is pointing at. There, in minuscule letters, is etched JOSEPH DOGLIO. I say his name out loud. My face becomes red as I try desperately to fight back the tears. I had searched earlier and, frustrated, had been unable to find it among the almost three hundred names. She found it immediately.

"This is what I came here to see," I say, my body trembling and my shaking voice almost inaudible.

"And you have shown me so much more, thank you."

I realize I am standing alone in front of the window. She had left me to bear witness to the names of the *Angel* crew. Dallas Hawkins, Earl Hart, and the others were easy to find now. Sniffling, I turn to find her back at the pew, staring at the alter and holding again the locket in her tiny hands. I smile at her and thanked her again for showing me Joseph's name on the window.

She extends her hands toward me. "Give me your

hand," she nods as to say it is okay. I place my hand in hers and feel an incredible and indescribable warmth surge through my body. The heat burns my hand feeling as though the skin is scorching off from her touch. Instinctively, I try my best to pull my hand away from the flaming grip. But, her hands are like a crucible of fire and I can not free myself.

"You must believe to know," she says, her voice echoing through the hallowed walls of the church. "I have shown you much as I was very close to Joseph, it is you who will come to know the rest." Her grip lightens and she releases my hand.

I look at my hand expecting it to hurt, yet amazingly I feel nothing.

At this point, I know I was destined to meet her here. The strange occurrences had not been unplanned. I am amazed at the tranquility and peace in her eyes, but I cannot understand who she was. "Is she an angel?" Believing myself to be crazy, I hesitantly dismiss the thought. She looks at me and as if again reading my thoughts and whispers slowly one word.

"Believe."

We leave the church. She offers to drive Allen and me back to the hotel in Cambridge and I gratefully accept.

The forty minute drive from Anstey to Cambridge seems shorter than before, yet the only words spoken was a question she directed to me. "You have been praying for a small child?" With amazement, I searched her gentle eyes.

"How did you know?" I was astonished by her question. Her answer was more stunning than her question. I turn toward the window in silence and awe. Only the humming of the engine can be heard in the car. Allen notices when we get back to the car that something has happened between us and reverently sits quietly in the back seat.

When we arrive at the driveway of the hotel I ask,

"Will I see you again this trip?" I have a feeling we wouldn't, but I still hoped.

"You will see me again sometime, I'm sure." Her smile returns calming me from the earlier events.

"Thank you so much for everything you showed us today, I learned so much," I say in appreciation.

"Yes, thank you, Anne, I mean Emily," Allen stammers.

"You're welcome, it was my pleasure," she says waving as she drove away.

As we entered the hotel lobby, I turn to Allen, "Why did you accidently call her Anne?"

"Oh, I don't know, I'm old and she looked like a woman I used to know named Anne," he chuckles to himself.

"Well," I say exhausted from the day. "I'm going to take a nap."

"See you later, Sonny," Allen retorts.

The roll of film jingles in my pocket with the

loose change as I walk up the stairs to my room. I can hardly wait to have it developed.

I sit on my bed pulling my shoes off, my feet aching from the walks.

My wife's voice suddenly rings through my head recalling what she had said before I left for England. "This trip will be good for you...I have this strange feeling..." Kathryn's pleasant voice had trailed off that night.

"Had Emily been an angel?" The thought crosses my mind again before I drift into dreams.

Rosemary and John Cosco at Woodman Inn

John Cosco - Don Gaddo at
Cambridge Military Cemetery

Ed and Bea Soule in 1944

Ed and Bea Soule today

Don Gaddo - Bob Hart at Cambridge Military
Cemetery

Allen Ostrom
Tail Gunner 398th Bomb Group and special friend

Members of 398th Bomb Group

Hank Rudow (left) and friends

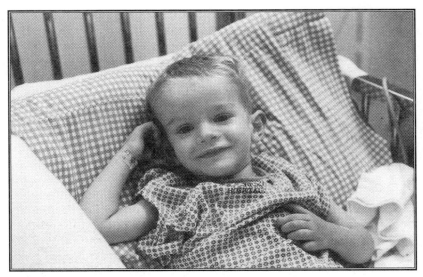

Connor Dahm in recovery room, July 10, 2000
*It is only with the heart that one can see rightly; what is
essential is invisible to the eye.*
-ANTOINE DE SAINT-EXUPERY
-The Little Prince

St. George's Church
Anstey, England

Footpath to Pains End

Chapter Seven

A Kiss, A Parachute, and A Little Boy

An eyelid flutters and glancing at the bold red digits on the clock, I realize its almost 8:00 A.M. in the morning. Sitting straight up in bed, I discover I had fallen asleep intending on taking a small nap and instead slept through to the morning still wearing the blue trousers from the window dedication. I remember waking several times during the night, my thoughts returning to the mysterious, Emily. The encounter had left me unsettled and pondering her identity. Not only did I continue to relive the experience but I suddenly realize I had no way to find her. She left no address nor did she leave a phone number. Stretching my arms as I awoke from my long and needed slumber, I quickly shower knowing that the tour bus departs for Duxford Imperial

War Museum in under an hour. Seeing John Cosco, Allen, and Ed Soule loading the bus from my window, I rush down the stairs regretfully not having the time to visit the continental breakfast bar.

"We missed seeing you last night," Rosemary, John's wife, says cheerfully.

"Yes, I meant to come downstairs to talk to everyone in the parlor last night, but I accidentally fell asleep."

"That happens to me all the time," Allen laughs adjusting his seatbelt. "My old body thinks it's night all the time these days. I'm just always tuckered out," he and John chuckle again.

I can tell they are poking a little fun at the idea that a younger man could not stay awake long enough to surpass a man in his eighties. I sheepishly smile and sit in my seat.

Driving to the museum, Allen comments on the roads.

"Some roads here in England are called lanes. Funny name eh?" he chuckles.

Lanes are long, narrow and, as I come to discover, not really equipped for large tour buses. The Imperial War Museum is just outside Cambridge. This meant that there were several lanes to be taken to the museum. As we near Duxford, the bus driver suddenly stops the bus. I sit up in my seat and looked ahead gasping. The lane had turned into a dirt and gravel road seeming to be only as wide as a bike path. I assume we would walk to the museum from here, yet some of the older passengers would have some trouble on the steep slant of the hill, so the bus driver pauses most likely running in his mind what to do.

I keep my eyes looking straight out the window. The weather is cloudy and gray again, and I hope it will not rain before we reach the museum.

A clanking noise can be heard in the distance. Since most of the windows on the bus had been open to vent air as we were stopped, people begin to curiously mumble, wondering where the clanking is coming from. It sounded to me to be the clanking and ringing of an old bike I used to have when I delivered newspapers as a kid. "Ole red," I remember. "It sounds just like her."

Some of the group want to step outside, as the driver thought of what to do, and so I join them wanting to see what is coming down the lane. Lo and behold the clanking got louder and the figure of a small boy on a bicycle comes into view. I giggle to myself, knowing I am right at guessing the mysterious sound. He is flying on his bicycle down the hill, peddling faster and faster, his cheeks flushed with perspiration. Red and yellow streamers hang out of the handlebars of the bike looking festive and cheerful to the eye. I don't know where he is so urgently going, but it is a sight to see this determined ten year old looking boy, furiously peddling and bouncing up and down the hills.

The bus driver must have seen the little boy,

because he begins to laugh and calling everyone into the bus, says that if a little boy can make it, so shall we.

The bus did make it to the museum bouncing its passengers like pieces of popcorn and making loud engine groans as it pushed its way up the hill. Once again filing off the tour bus, the first thing I notice about the Duxford Imperial War Museum is how enormous it is. There are five giant airplane hangers, an American Air Museum, and several separate buildings housing newly built coffee shops and snack bars. The tour's first stop is at the American Air Museum where there will be memorabilia, planes, and pictures from World War II to be seen. Ed Soule walks quickly ahead of me, rushing to see the planes.

I wonder if he had seen them since the war. This seems to be one of the most important parts of the trip for him. Not only has he come back and seen where he had flown at Base 131, he is now seeing a B-17 just like his.

The monstrosity of the B-17 Flying Fortress is

incomprehensible. I stood eyes wide, mouth agape until I feel a nudge at my shoulder. "Ain't she a beauty," Allen's thick accent now evident in his speech. "They were so intimidating to me then and still scare the dickens out of me now," he says smiling in awe.

I smiled back at Allen wondering what it would have been like to be handed at nineteen or twenty the controls of such a remarkable machine.

Ed Soule had moved from examining the planes to the displays of bombshells, uniforms, and parachutes. I walk over to the display admiring its historical contents."Ever go down in a parachute?" he says interrupting my thoughts.

"No, sir, can't say that I have," I politely reply.

"Can be very painful, I'll tell you." he says laughing. "I know first hand what can go wrong with a parachute."

I look at him wondering what is so humorous, but I do not have to wonder long before a story is started.

"I was a ball turret gunner, one of the men who stays cramped up in that little Plexiglass bubble in the underbelly of the plane. It was not the best position to be in. You were in the bomb area and at any moment something could go wrong and poof, there you went too," his voice became serious. "On one mission, I was shot up pretty badly in my leg, and one of my crew members treated the wounds taking my bulky sheepskin lined pants off and covering me with a blanket. I remember thinking that I wanted to go home so my mom could bandage me up properly. I loved my crew, but none of them were doctors," he laughed again. "I was still in my parachute straps because I always needed to be prepared to bail out if the plane was shot up by enemy fire. Well, the plane took a near direct hit and began losing altitude. I knew we had to bail out. Not having the time to put my pants on, I filed out with the rest of the crew." A grimace crossed his face. "Unfortunately I didn't think to adjust my chute straps compensating for the removal of my heavy sheepskin lined flight britches. When I pulled my parachute cord the loose fitting strap catapulted into my groin area. The straps became tighter and tighter," he continued. "Pardon me for saying this aloud but it felt as though my testicles were being crushed by a cast iron anvil." I winced at the thought.

"As I floated to the ground a British Spitfire circled the crew. He was obviously reporting our location so we could be picked up and given needed medical attention.

"I was in terrible pain from the wounds in my leg but the straps of that parachute was causing unbearable pain to the most treasured parts of my body," he grins and adds, "you know what I mean."

"I signaled to the pilot in the Spitfire to shoot me." Soule pretended to be shooting a .50 caliber machine gun. His arms shook as he imitated the bouncing and rattling of his weapon. "I honestly wanted him to put me out of my misery. I remember thinking this is it, I'm going to be dead from a parachute strap to the groin," he chuckled. "I'm glad to this day that the pilot could not understand the young man pointing at his chest and wincing in pain." He smiles.

"I'm glad you are able to laugh at that experience now," I say grinning. "I don't think I would have been able to."

"You bet, parachutes can be dangerous," he winks. "They aren't as innocent as they look in that glass case."

We both step away from the case and split. He went to examine the first aid display booth, and I went to the section of war guns. I rub my thigh and shiver. If ever I have an idea to do some skydiving, Ed's story changed my ambitions.

I came to the glass case holding the war guns. Machine guns, pistols, and all kinds of old looking weapons rested silently and untouched since 1945.

Bob Hart stood gazing over the case, his eyes shifting to the automatic machine guns.

"Oh, the glory," he mutters to himself.

"Pardon me?" I say wondering if he is speaking to me.

"Oh, sorry I am just thinking of a memory," he said under his breath.

I can tell he wants to talk, so I ask him, "Did you ever get to use one of these in combat?"

"Not exactly, you see I was a co-pilot in the 600th squadron so most of my attention was focused on flying the plane. I always wanted to shoot a German aircraft from a B-17 though and once I had my chance but not from the plane.

A German aircraft flew over Base 131 and I happened to be near the field. I instinctively grabbed a machine gun much like the ones in the case and fired every round at the plane. Although I never even touched the beast, I never took any greater pleasure in firing at the Germans than when I did than during that one moment." A proud smile crosses his face and understanding what the moment must have been, I return his smile.

"You are a good man. I wanted you to know that."
I walk away from that conversation feeling that a part of
a soldier's memory has entered my heart.

I decide to walk out of the steel building and
outside for some air. I notice out of the corner of my eye
the red and yellow streamers on the handlebars of the
little boy's bike. It is leaning against the side of the
building and I anxiously begin looking for the little boy
on the grounds. I wonder who he is here to visit, or
maybe he just came to explore like most boys his age like
to do. I notice groups of veterans walking around often
stopping to talk. The edges of a cream skirt catch my
attention, but I know it can not be Emily. I wonder if she
might come to the museum or even to the concluding
dinner tonight at the hotel. Today is the last day I will
have the chance to see her, but I know, in my heart, I will
not.

People dressed in traditional World War II

uniforms walk the grounds. I notice a pilot in a brown suit, ribbons decorating his uniform, a woman in a white Red Cross Hostess sheath, and a women in blue.

The blue uniform is worn by a woman portraying a World War II WASP. A smart blue jacket overlaps neatly pressed bell bottom slacks. A white blouse offset the attractive blue beret that is smartly placed over her flowing auburn hair.

The Red Cross hostess wears a World War II knee length white frock with the noticeable Red Cross emblem emblazoned over her heart. A wide smile adorns her face.

The uniformed pilot is dressed in a snappy officers uniform complete with the floppy Air Force cap. If I didn't know better I would have sworn I had been catapulted back in time.

I keep my eyes peeled for the little boy, my curiosity as to why he is here becoming overwhelming. I suddenly feel the presence of a person next to me and turn to face a young blonde woman dressed in the traditional WASP uniform of navy blue slacks and WASP beret.

"Excuse me sir, but I wanted to give you this." She leans over and kisses me on the cheek. I blush, surprised at what just happened. "That man over there wanted you to know what it felt like to be kissed during the war," she laughs and points at Allen who pretends we aren't looking at him and then teasingly waves.

I thank her and then grinning at Allen I salute him and begin walking to the group of veterans still outside. I move my hand to the spot where she had kissed me. I touch my finger to the red lipstick covering my cheek. I wish Kathryn was here to experience all of these exciting, somewhat embarrassing moments.

Just then, a small figure can be seen walking among the crowd. I recognize the little boy almost immediately. He is wearing old tennis shoes and a tan T-shirt almost blending in with the men in tan uniforms scattered around the base. The look on his face is one of curiosity and amazement. With his big brown eyes, he seems to gaze up at the old veterans almost knowing what they had been through so long ago. These were true heroes in his mind. They fought in the giant aircraft he was seeing and used the guns perched in the glass cases. I can sense the battles becoming alive in the child's imagination. I watch the little boy and feel that in a way he knows and understands more about these men than I, fifty-two years older, understand. I hear John' familiar voice approaching and turn to face him and his wife.

"Enjoying yourself here?" he asks.

"Yes, it is so interesting to see everything still intact and preserved," I say glancing across their shoulders for the little boy.

I excuse myself as the group begins to speak of the differences in German Aircraft and wandered the grounds looking for the lad. He has disappeared.

Wally Blackwell, the tour coordinator, began

rounding the group up and warning that the bus is leaving for Anstey in fifteen minutes. I dismiss the little boy's whereabouts and walk toward the bus.

After climbing onto the bus and sitting at a window, I look to where the bike had been propped against the building. It is gone. The bus is loaded and the entire tour group accounted for. Engines start as I continue looking out the window making a memory of the war museum in my head. I hear a women yell, "Look, there he is again!"

Everyone leans over to the windows as the bus begins to move and the little boy races alongside peddling even harder than I had seen before. The yellow and red streamers whipped in the wind as his flushed face smiles at the people peering out of the bus. He continues up the huge hill, the bus driver had been so afraid to ascend, determined to make it without stopping. Some people on the bus cheer at the little boy's accomplishment, turning to each other saying what a strong lad he is.

I knew then why he had come and who he had come to visit. He had come to see the old heroes, those who are sitting proudly on this very bus. He, in his young mind, had known they were coming after seeing the bus and knew they would be watching as he sped courageously past them on his bike. He wanted to be a hero and in a sense, he had proved himself with the cheering and clapping sounding from the old heroes on the bus. The bike turns down another gravel lane and disappears in a cloud of chalky dust. Suddenly I recall a photograph of Joseph sitting on a bicycle much like the one that has disappeared down the lane. Joseph, at the time of the photograph, was about the same age as the boy and Joseph's bike had streamers dangling from the handlebars.

I turn to the window trying to catch one last glimpse of the young boy. Through the dust I see him stop and wave, not to the group, but to me. "Joseph?" I whisper.

We return to Anstey one final time to visit the window and take a group picture. Ed, John, and Allen briefly touch the window each saying something silently and then return outside to gather together.

I stay longer at the window, Joseph's name boldly staring back at me. I am mesmerized by the doves, the fire, and the B-17's symbolically used in the window. I say a silent prayer for peace and walk solemnly out to the rest of the group. After the picture is taken, I walk quickly to the oak tree wanting to see it once more and notice something I had not seen yesterday with Emily. She had been leaning against the back of the tree so I was unable to see the initials JD and AH carved in the side. My eyes widen and I feel a rush of emotions flood my mind. Joseph and Anne, I thought. "This had been where Joseph and Anne had come, maybe for the last time." I place my index finger in the initials. I slowly trace the letters JD and then moving my hand below I repeat the same slow process with the carvings of AH. A sudden surge of emotion, anxiety, and warmth fills my senses. My knees become shaky and seem weakened by my discovery. I brace myself against the tree and slowly kneel on one knee. With my room key, I loosened the soil where I had been standing. Scooping a handful of black dirt, I place it in my handkerchief and neatly tie it in a secure knot. This is the soil where Joseph and Anne once stood. This small handful of history belongs to me.

I hear Allen's husky voice calling out my name and tell him I am on my way.

When we reach the hotel, I go back to my room to prepare for the concluding dinner of the trip. I find a small brown cardboard box at the reception desk and I gently place the soil from Anstey in the container. The box and its contents are more priceless than any expensive piece of jewelry it had before contained.

I begin thinking how I will miss all of my new friends, Ed, John, and Allen. They have been a comfort and a blessing in disguise on the trip. Each person on the tour had their own stories to tell and I am sure I have missed many along the way, yet I came across so many heartfelt lessons and triumphs that I can be thankful to have heard. The "Farewell to England" dinner is set for 7:00 P.M.

Entering the Orchard Room for the last time I find John and Rosemary Cosco. Together with several others from the 398th we enjoy our final evening in England. We reminisce our exciting days and eventful evenings. Each story is more enjoyable than the last.

After dinner Wally Blackwell and Allen Ostrom, a tail gunner in the 603rd squadron, speak to the gathering of people. Wally talks of days gone by and then thanks everyone for making the trip enjoyable.

Allen Ostrom talks of several specific memories of the war and provides a moving and emotional farewell speech. There is not a dry eye in the room. As Allen finishes, Dick Frazier, the designated choir director for the veterans of the 398th suddenly begins to sing a solo.

The room was hushed as gentle sobbing is heard from across the ballroom. Then a woman begins to sing and then another. Soon the voices begin to grow in number.

As everyone sings I listen. Looking at Allen, Ed, and John, my new friends, I wonder if this will be their last time together. I am saddened by the thought. I glance at Bob Hart and Wally Blackwell. I wonder if they will see each other again? My eyes survey the room. They are all singing now, their voices raised high in acclamation.

My eyes return to John Cosco, Joseph's friend and the last living member of the *Angel* crew. I study his face and his features. I move by his side and put my arms around him and hold him for several seconds. Then, without saying a word he smiles at me in understanding.

Returning his smile I gently remove a tear from my eye. I take his hand and join in the singing. . .

   . . .*And we'll take a cup o' kindness yet*

For auld lang syne! . . .

Chapter Eight

Future Generations and a Roll of Film

The idea of having to return to North Carolina wanders into my head as I begin packing my things into my worn brown leather suitcase again. My flight isn't scheduled to leave until mid-afternoon and I plan to eat lunch for a final time with my new friends. I begin to think about the men that I have been privileged to know during this short week. Walking downstairs to the dining room area I join John, Allen, Bob, and Ed at a long rectangular table neatly set for lunch. Between conversations of battles won and plans after they return to the states, I glance at the individuals at my table. Directly across from me is the intent John Cosco, who knows why I came to England and who knew Joseph as the young man who vibrantly played his worn saxophone before missions. They had been close friends, and he had been the only person remaining in the crew who could best tell his story. He had done more than share Joseph's story; he had shared with me a part of himself I felt he hadn't spoke of in years. Sitting on the right side of John is Ed whose expression is one of interest in what is being said at the table. From the beginning of the trip, I had wondered about him and his wife Bea. They are an intriguing couple and I came to discover that their vibrancy and enthusiasm for life revived the group.

Bob Hart slowly approaches the table sitting down and ordering a water. His legs are weak, yet he walks with his head held high as if he were still waiting to salute a commanding officer. I recall the day I first saw this man when visiting Base 131. He was struggling to climb up the embankment on his hands and knees wanting to reach the monument without assistance. His point was proven that day. Even the weakest shall overcome the impossible boundaries if having the strongest of heart. Bob, chattering to Allen about the menu, has taught me a lesson that day about continuing life through strength. This strength could not solely be physical, as evident by his feeble body, it has to consist of emotional determination as well. He smiles at me, as if knowing I am thinking of him, and continues his conversation with the table.

I eat a few bites of my cold turkey sandwich and looking across the table notice an animated Allen telling a story with his southern accent while occasionally missing the pronunciations of "r". I laugh quietly to myself making sure no one has noticed and realize the humor Allen has added to my trip. His mismatched socks and continuous hearty laugh could always make me smile. The emotional time we spent at the Woodman Inn, my tea in hand and he with his pint of Guinness, can never be forgotten. It is through him that I discover how important it is to the veterans to be remembered. They sacrificed their youth so that future generations could have the rights and freedoms they deserved. He wanted younger generations and new generations to always remember what I could never forget after taking this trip. So many people had lost their lives while stationed in England during the war. So many of these people had been friends of these veterans sitting before me.

Bob's voice from days earlier echoes in my head, "Son, do you know what it's like to lose someone? To be helpless and afraid and at moments your entire life flashed before your eyes?" I hadn't been able to answer then, because I honestly didn't know what that must have felt like. Now, after becoming friends with the four men at my table, I feel as though I had a better understanding of them, their experience and the tragedies of war. I suddenly feel a pride for these men as I stare at their weathered faces wrinkled from years of work and memories. It's difficult for me to relate to that tragic part of their lives, yet at times when they were sharing those moments with me, I felt as though I could be in battle along side them if asked.

Plates become clean and cleared from the table as I realize the lunch is coming to an end. There is a little hesitation by the men to stand up from the table since no one wanted to initiate the end of such a memorable event.

After endless anticipation and excitement, the week has drawn to a friendly closing. I stand from my chair and extend my hand to Bob Hart first. He shakes it, his grip stronger than I had expected with an encouraging smile strewn across his face. Next, I say my good-byes to John Cosco thanking him for being an important part of my cousin's life. He speaks clearly in my ear as he embraces me. "It was an honor to fly with such an incredible man and talented saxophone player. He helped us to be at ease before the missions, just as you have during this trip through your interest and concern." Astonished and honored that I could have been of any consolation to these men, I returned his embrace. Ed and Bea jokingly warn me that I can not be rid of them just yet because they are on the same returning flight.

I smile and turn to Allen in his worn tree-bark brown trousers and wrinkled white collared shirt. He had a kind expression on his face as he spoke to the others. He is one of the veterans who had visible scars of war evident in the empty sleeve that was carefully tucked and pinned under at the seam. We have a bond that had formed from the unforgettable experience we shared with the mysterious woman known only to us as Emily. I hated having to leave Allen, but I know we will keep in touch somehow after we return home. He takes me aside from the rest of the group and placing his arm on my shoulder says, "I cannot explain in words what it has meant having someone to listen to me this week. I needed a confidant and friend to get me through the tormenting memories that war can bring back into an old man's heart. You have been both to me this week." His seriousness catches me off guard as he seems to be a changed person from his usual goofy grin and southern drawl. I thank him for his company and for the opportunity to experience through him a side of the war I would have never been able to comprehend. We promise to keep in touch and I say again my farewell.

I step up the spiral, marble staircase a final time to gather my suitcase. Taking a taxi from the hotel to Heathrow Airport, I mumble softly a farewell to England. I know deep down that I will never again have the opportunity to come to visit the rolling green countryside and the quaintness of Cambridge in my lifetime. I am at peace now with my cousin's memory. I know who he had been and whose lives he had touched during that short period at Base 131.

The airport is busting at the seams with people hurriedly running to gates, some gathering around family members now leaving for trips and some anxiously awaiting those arriving from various exotic places. I imagine my wife standing at the gate when I, too, arrive home. The line of international travelers boarding my plane is long as I approach the gate.

Setting my briefcase, containing all of my memorabilia from the trip, I see something out of the corner of my eye. Still bent over, my eyes caught the sight of a long, flowing cream skirt nearing the chrome check-in counter. I stand frozen in my place in line, unable to move thinking of the possibility that I will see Emily before I leave. Much to my disappointment, as I glance up at the woman wearing the cream skirt, I know immediately that it isn't she. The kind smile and warm aura of Emily' presence is unmistakable and clearly the younger woman at the counter is not Emily. Sighing at the idea that I will never see Emily again, I move my way up the line and into the airplane once again attempting to become situated in the small cushioned seats allotted to coach passengers.

The flight home seems longer than the one taken a week earlier. Ed and his wife sit closer to the back of the plane, so I don't have the opportunity to speak to them during the flight. I didn't feel the same anxiety that had surged through my body last week in anticipation for England. Now, I feel a sense of peace and relaxation knowing I have learned through this one-week trip more about my cousin and the war then I could have gained from all the books and letters read in a lifetime. I spend the hours in the plane thinking of the church and of the stained glass window, which has been the highlight of the trip. Opening the John Grisham book, I attempt to read through chapters but instead find myself focusing on my wandering thoughts.

The plane arrives on schedule and after hugging Ed and Bea good-bye, I discover my cheerful wife waiting at the end of the ramp.

"I'm so glad you're home, I can't wait to hear all about the trip," she says kissing me on the cheek.

"You won't believe half the things I'm going to tell you dear, it was an incredible experience. . .

everything was."

We move to the baggage claim area casually talking about the flight and the southern dinner that awaits me at home. I carry my weary body into my wife's car and we drive towards Chapel Hill. I am happy to see the tree lined streets again. The atmosphere is so different from England, yet I am content on being home. A small red convertible filled with teenagers speeds past us just before we reach our street. I can hear the music blaring even with our car windows rolled up. Screams can be heard by girls laughing at the male driver's suave ability to pass and speed recklessly past the traffic.

I can sense by the look on Kathryn's face that she too has also noticed the wild teenagers. I think about what Allen had said about the younger generations forgetting about them. I wonder if the kids in the convertible will ever experience anything like what I had during the trip. As they speed past older people, I secretly want to know if they even took notice of who they may be passing. Younger generations seem to worry older generations sometimes. The knowledge and opportunities of today's youth far exceeds what previous generations or I ever dreamt of. It's amazing how much we learn from each other. My wife has been looking over at me for a few minutes and interrupts my thoughts. "What are you thinking about?' she inquisitively asks. "You are staring out into space."

"Oh, nothing really. Just thinking about young people and old people and how different we can be, but how alike we truly are. I kind of wish there had been some younger people on the tour to experience the emotion and share that feeling with older generations."

"I'm sure there will be someone who will share it with them," she smiles winking at me. I do tend to tell some good stories in my day. I will go back and share most of them with the students who would be interested in listening.

Pulling into the driveway, I feel a little relieved to

be home again. The house is clean, as always, and the familiar smell of mashed potatoes is wafted in my direction as my wife jolts past me remembering something left cooking in the oven. Everything is set on the table and after sitting down in silence for a few minutes the conversation begins. I share with her my times with Allen, Ed, John, and Bob. It is like they are coming to life again as I talk about their different personalities and different experiences during the war.

After dinner, I sit in my oversized chair catching up in the news with my paper and occasionally looking at the television. I dread unpacking all of my things and instead procrastinate leaving the chore until tomorrow. My wife is sprawled on the couch facing my chair with her tattered book in hand and the dim light of the lamp reflecting in her glasses. It is as if I had never left my quaint little home in North Carolina. Everything is back to normal. The next morning I awoke in my own bed, which is larger and softer than those at the Crowne Plaza

Hotel. My wife is already awake and cooking in the kitchen. The suitcases sit in my room staring at me. I shrug, secretly hoping that Kathryn will unpack them before I have gotten the chance to. I go into the kitchen to my smiling wife who informs me that the grass needs to be cut, the bushes need trimmed, and that the back doorknob is jammed. I laugh hugging her and say, "Wow, you sure must have missed me being here, sweetie."

She kindly grumbles, "Yeah, things seem to break more around here when you are gone."

I move to the front porch grabbing my unfinished book from the front table. The skies are that same Carolina blue and the weather is sunny and humid. I watch people stroll past my front porch. One of my favorite things to do is people watch. Trying to guess where each person is from and where he or she is going can captivate me for hours. Sometimes I wave, smile and talk to the passing strangers. Today, I become enveloped in my book, thinking about the sunshine and how perfect my week abroad had ended.

I hear the shuffling of feet behind me knowing that it is Kathryn and I pretend that I don't know she is coming.

"Boo," she says smiling. "I started to unpack your things since you seemed to have conveniently forgotten to. I found a roll of film in your blue slacks, the ones I told you to bring," she says feeling proud of her foresight.

I drop the book from the chair. I hadn't remembered the finished roll of film from that day at the church. I had thought yesterday during the flight that I had misplaced it at the hotel.

"Where did you put it?" I gasp anxious at the thought of getting it developed.

"It's on your dresser. Why are you in such a rush all of a sudden?"

I couldn't hear what she was saying; I had already

bolted inside in search of the film. In one of those pictures I know there is a picture of Emily. Something inside of me is telling me that it is urgent that I see this picture. Leaving my wife speechless on the porch, I jump into the car and drove to the one-hour developing place. My hand is shaking as I fill out the form and promise the guy I will return in precisely one hour. I, then drive around the block a few times listening to Glen Miller and anticipating the pictures. The clock seems to sense I am waiting and the hour slowly creeps by. Finally, I go to pick them up; the young man behind the counter giving me a strange look as I grab the bag, pay and hustle to the car.

I wait an extra five minutes to open them when I am once again sitting on the porch with Kathryn.

The pictures of Cambridge briefly bring me back to the days earlier when I had been walking the streets myself. Each photograph had a story but it wasn't until I reach the end of the sequence of pictures when I see the oak tree, the airstrip, and most importantly, Emily. She hadn't known I had photographed her as she is looking out at something, her auburn hair strewn across her face. She is looking downward at her locket, but this time unlike any other time I had been in her presence, it is open. I notice it is completely open and two minuscule pictures were almost visible in the photograph. Going inside, I retrieve a dusty magnifying glass, its handle worn from past years of boy scouting. I had wondered who she kept in her locket and now maybe I could find out.

A deep gasp escapes my lips and I toss the picture down running into the other room to recover another picture.

My eyes began watering when I realize who was in her locket all this time. His peaceful, intent brown eyes stared back at me. Holding the picture I had discovered in the tattered suitcase months earlier, I realize it is the same photograph small and carefully placed in the right side of the locket.

It is Joseph.

"How could this be?" I wonder my hand brushing away new tears.

On the left side of the locket is a picture of a woman. That woman I know could only be Anne. Looking through the magnifying glass I can see her features. The same warm smile and auburn hair as Emily.

"That's impossible, Anne is not alive anymore. . .or is she?"

Kathryn came in the room questioning all the commotion earlier with the film.

"What is going on? Are you going to show me the pictures?. . .Honey, are you crying?"

"Nothing's going on dear," I stumble on the words. "Yes, I will show you everything and I'm crying because I have finished my quest to know Joseph. Somehow, I was shown and felt a part of him through the one person he truly loved in England. It's all very strange, dear."

Looking puzzled she comes to my side.

I laugh, "Now, I have some really good stories to share with the students and people passing by."

"Well, you can start by telling them to me," she stubbornly says still looking confused.

"Well, it all starts with a letter and a locket. . ." The gleam of interest sparkling in her eyes secretly told me that this is what Joseph would have wanted. The chance to have a love story unforgotten by time and sparking the mind and imagination to wonder. . . "Do angels really exist?"

I can only hope. . . and *BELIEVE.*

The Miracle and the Child

During our return to Cambridge, Emily asked a question of me. "You have been praying for a small child?"

My response was silence. My reaction was to face the window on the passenger side of the car. I was in awe of this gracious and congenial woman. How did she know?

In 1957 I attended Illinois State University. My roommate was Hugo Dahm, a slender, athletic young man from Downers Grove, Illinois. He was dating his high school sweetheart, Jean. In time the three of us became close friends.

The college years past, we found ourselves going our separate ways and eventually we lost track of each other. In the early spring of 2000 a letter appeared in my mail box. The return address bore the name, Hugo Dahm. Excitedly, I opened the slightly creased white envelope. The brief note simply read, "If you were my roommate at Illinois State, please call me." The short note was signed, Hugo.

Kathryn and I did call and we made arrangements to meet Hugo and his wife, in Morris, Illinois. In two short hours we exchanged years of memories. It was one of many highlights in my life.

Before leaving Jean told us the heartbreaking story of their two year old grandson, Connor. He was born with what appeared to be an incurable heart defect. At the age of two Connor had undergone four surgeries and his health had not allowed him to enjoy or understand the pleasures of childhood.

Jean told me of her pilgrimage to Medjugorje in Croatia. Medjugorje is where Mary, the Blessed Virgin Mother, continues to appear to several children as she has done since 1981. Jean prayed intensely for Connor during her visit and she has prayed earnestly ever since.

Hugo, interrupting Jean, explained that Connor was scheduled for an operation in July of 2000. If successful the operation would be the first step in Connors struggle to be an active, healthy child. If it failed, the prospects for his future were dim.

Jean became emotional and apologized, but no apology was needed. Hugo looked into the distance and said. "Spider," a nickname I had earned years earlier, "I just want to be a grandfather who some day has an opportunity to play catch with his grandson."

Now, since our reunion, Kathryn and I have been praying for Connor. We keep him close to our hearts.

What I did not write about in the previous chapters was a brief exchange Emily and I had before saying good-bye in front of the Crowne Plaza Hotel.

"Your question," I asked her, "about the prayers for a small child."

Nodding her head, she said, "Yes, he is a beautiful child."

"How is it that you know him?" I inquired. Then pausing I added, "I seem to have asked that question many times today."

She seemed calm and composed, "What is it you want for this child?"

"I want him to live, to be loved."

"I see," she pondered my answer. "You want him to live but what is life? If he lives and remains on this earth will he not be loved? If it is the will of God that the child journey to a new home, does he not have life and love as well?"

Her answer to my question was in the form of another question. I sat in silence considering my answer to her. The words that came to my mind made me acutely aware that I was a mere human.

Somewhat embarrassed at my inability to find the proper words I said, "Well, you see Emily, Hugo wants to play catch with his grandson." A nervous grin crossed my face, "And I pray my friend will have the pleasure of sharing that joy."

She smiled. She had a warmth about her that pierced my very soul. She removed one hand from the steering wheel and placed it on top of mine. The intensity of the warmth in her hand seemed to grow with each passing second. The feeling was incredible.

Finally, removing her hand, she glanced in my

direction. She caressed the locket that hung loosely from her neck. The moment will live with me forever.

"Baseball! What would you Yanks do without baseball?" Then softly, "Tell the boys grandparents to buy him a glove and a saxophone."

* * *

On July 5, 2000 Connor entered the surgery ward of a hospital in Chicago, Illinois. Several hours later he emerged full of surgical tubes and monitoring devices.

Jean, his grandmother, was given an opportunity to visit the child for a brief moment. She cried, not because of the tubes and monitors, but something told her that Connor, by some miracle, had crossed a giant hurdle. She saw the color of his skin was not pale and ashen; he seemed to radiate with life. She had no doubt that the color of her grandson's skin was not a result of the bright orange sun in the heavens, but from the Son, who had answered her prayers.

Now, as I prepare to write my final words, I pause to look out the window. The North Carolina sun is shining brightly and the striking blue of the Carolina sky leaves me in deep thought.

The sky speaks to me with it's brilliance. Walking to the window I search the blue skies for a friend.

"Thank you Anne, or Emily, or whoever you are. Thank you for giving my friend, Hugo, the opportunity to play catch with his grandson." Then with a smile I add, "Don't worry about the saxophone. I'll give it to him personally.

Something envelopes me. I feel a presence around me. I turn to look over my shoulder.

"Thank you Joseph." and then I add, "do you still have your St. Christopher Medal?"

* * *

How like an angel came I down.

– Thomas Traherne

Wonder

The Stained Glass Window Order Form

Use this convenient order form to order additional copies
of
The Stained Glass Window

Please Print:

Name_____

Address_____

City_____ **State**_____

Zip_____

Phone(   )_____

_____ copies of book @ $17.95 each $ _____

Postage and handling @ $3.00 per book $ _____

NC residents add 1.08% tax $ _____

Total amount enclosed $ _____

Make checks payable to Don Gaddo

Send to Don Gaddo
P. O. Box 773 • Chapel Hill, NC 27514